‖‖‖ ‖ ‖‖‖‖‖‖‖‖‖‖‖‖‖‖‖‖‖‖‖‖‖‖ ‖ ‖‖

◁ **W9-BLO-977**

"I can't wear this," Hallie whispered

She couldn't wear the beautiful engagement ring, she shouldn't, but she couldn't take her eyes from it. And she couldn't keep her heart from breaking over the gesture.

"Please...take it off," Hallie begged.

"It's tradition," Wes insisted.

"This isn't a real marriage," she got out hastily.

She couldn't bear the new sharpness in his dark eyes and her gaze fled his. She pulled her hand from his and immediately took hold of the ring to take it off.

Wes caught her hands before she could remove the ring....

What kind of man makes the perfect husband?

A man with a big heart and strong arms—someone tough but tender, powerful yet passionate....

And where can such a man be found?

In our brand-new miniseries:

Marriages made on the ranch...

Look for these Western weddings throughout 2000, in Harlequin Romance®.

THE MARRIAGE BARGAIN

Susan Fox

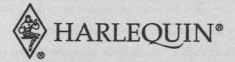

TORONTO • NEW YORK • LONDON
AMSTERDAM • PARIS • SYDNEY • HAMBURG
STOCKHOLM • ATHENS • TOKYO • MILAN • MADRID
PRAGUE • WARSAW • BUDAPEST • AUCKLAND

If you purchased this book without a cover you should be aware that this book is stolen property. It was reported as "unsold and destroyed" to the publisher, and neither the author nor the publisher has received any payment for this "stripped book."

ISBN 0-373-03606-X

THE MARRIAGE BARGAIN

First North American Publication 2000.

Copyright © 2000 by Susan Fox.

All rights reserved. Except for use in any review, the reproduction or utilization of this work in whole or in part in any form by any electronic, mechanical or other means, now known or hereafter invented, including xerography, photocopying and recording, or in any information storage or retrieval system, is forbidden without the written permission of the publisher, Harlequin Enterprises Limited, 225 Duncan Mill Road, Don Mills, Ontario, Canada M3B 3K9.

All characters in this book have no existence outside the imagination of the author and have no relation whatsoever to anyone bearing the same name or names. They are not even distantly inspired by any individual known or unknown to the author, and all incidents are pure invention.

This edition published by arrangement with Harlequin Books S.A.

® and TM are trademarks of the publisher. Trademarks indicated with ® are registered in the United States Patent and Trademark Office, the Canadian Trade Marks Office and in other countries.

Visit us at www.eHarlequin.com

Printed in U.S.A.

CHAPTER ONE

HALLIE Corbett stared at the elderly man on the hospital bed. Grave illness hadn't dimmed Hank Corbett's harshness or the spite in his nature.

"You heard me," he panted. His gray eyes bore into hers. Gunmetal gray. Like a pair of Colts aimed at her brain, threatening her heart, imperiling the only life she'd ever known.

"You don't get a dime or a single Corbett investment. Candice gets all that."

Hallie was stoic. She'd learned early in life that showing emotion made her a target for attack. She sensed a follow-up to her grandfather's declaration. He always threw her a crumb, some insignificant scrap that kept her in the game.

He'd made her an emotional gambler. He'd barred her from his heart, but he always dangled something to keep her in range, to keep her hoping. And, like a dog about to starve to death, she always grabbed for the scrap. Though the crumb often turned out to be a mirage, it was the promise of a win that lured her.

And hope. Hope that the old man had let her stay on all these years because he had some fondness for the illegitimate child of his disgraced daughter.

Shaky promises and hope. Her real enemies, not

the old man on the bed or her cousin, Candice, the granddaughter Hank Corbett doted on.

Her voice was low, but loud enough for him to hear. "What about the ranch?"

"Four C's belongs to the Corbett worthy to carry on the legacy."

Hallie felt the familiar surge of jealousy and frustration, but was careful to keep her tone neutral. "Legacy means nothing to Candice. She'll have a buyer before they close your grave."

The words were brutal, but she ignored the shiver of guilt. She was fighting for her home, for the only thing she might ever have.

The old man's eyes sparkled with interest. He was like a wolf who'd caught a whiff of fresh blood. "You want it bad, don't you?"

Her lips went stiff with the effort to suppress a tremor of emotion. She didn't answer because they both knew she wanted the ranch. She loved the land. It didn't play favorites. It was no more harsh with her than it was with anyone else. She'd made peace with its wildness; it was in her blood.

Four C's Ranch was the only place she really did belong. And it wasn't the house or family that had given her a feeling of place, but the Texas soil itself and all that was nurtured by it. She'd held out this long for a chance at ownership. At least a piece.

The elderly man on the bed chuckled then choked, his face going red with the coughing spasm that silenced his mirth. Hallie made no move toward the bed because he'd reject her display of concern. He'd never allowed her to express even a hint of affection. He'd never offered her any.

When he recovered from the spasm, he closed his eyes. Hallie thought at first that he was dismissing her, but then his eyes opened and shot straight to hers. The gleam was back.

"You've been a shame on this family since your mama brought you home to me. But you're blood, however you got bred. Won't leave you a dime more than the first six months operating expenses, but you can have Four C's. *If* you get a husband before I die."

The words were so stupefying that Hallie forgot to mask her expression.

Hank Corbett smiled, a curve of pale lips that made him look truly evil. "Folks 'round here think you don't like men. Most aren't sure you're even female. Bastard's one thing, but I won't let a misfit inherit Four C's. Legacy can't live through a single woman who'll never breed heirs."

Hallie felt her head go light. The room actually started to spin.

"Had the lawyer put it in the will. Go see 'im if you got doubts. Make 'im show it to you." He expelled a weary breath. "Now get out of here. I need some rest."

Still in shock, Hallie turned and with rigid dignity walked from the room. When she reached the hall, she got only a few steps before she stopped and put out a hand to the wall for support. She was shaking all over.

She could have Four C's. Thirty thousand acres, shining in her mind like a massive jewel. It could be hers. The prize she'd hoped for, waited for and endured a lifetime of pain and deprivation to have a chance at. He'd willed it to her then yanked it away before she could reach for it.

A husband. Women like her didn't find husbands.

According to her grandfather, most people weren't sure she was female. Of course he'd say that. Anything to snatch away the last bit of confidence that had survived being bullied and shamed out of her.

And he'd accomplished his goal. Because the truth was, few people acknowledged her as a female because they never saw her act like one. She worked on the ranch as hard as a man, doing the same work and putting in the same grueling hours. She didn't own a dress, and couldn't remember when she'd last worn one. She'd never had a sweetheart or a date. With Candice around, she doubted men even noticed her.

You can have Four C's…if you get a husband….

Hank might as well demand that she fly to the moon.

Wes Lansing's Red Thorn Ranch was as large as the Four C's. The eastern boundary of the Red Thorn was also the western boundary of the Four C's. The Lansing and Corbett families had lived side by side for five generations; they'd been enemies for four.

At times, the enmity between the two families had been bloody, but for the past twenty years, it had settled into a wary calm that passed for civility.

Ironically, it was the warring history between the Corbetts and the Lansings that gave Hallie confidence. The feud had started over a parcel of land—a parcel that would be included in the Four C's land inheritance. If Hallie could meet the requirements to inherit the Four C's, the parcel would belong to her to do with as she pleased. If Wes Lansing was willing to barter with her to get it, she'd make certain he got the parcel.

Wes was a man just as hard and harsh as her grandfather, but he was known as a man of honor. He was honest and fair in his business dealings and with the people who worked for him.

But the biggest indication of his character was that Wes Lansing was the only eligible male in their part of Texas who was completely immune to her cousin Candice. In spite of the history between the Corbetts and Lansings, Candice had tried for years to snag his interest. And failed. He might be the one man Candice could never seduce away.

How bad did he want the parcel?

Two hours ago, they'd moved her grandfather into Intensive Care. Candice had banished her from the hospital, and Hallie was secretly relieved. Any time she could be spared Candice's venom was a blessing.

Especially now, when she didn't want to face her feelings about Hank Corbett's impending death. Because of the Will, she was taking what he would consider a disloyal step against him, and the knowledge made her queasy.

Hallie's heart thudded heavily in her chest as she felt the enormity of what she was about to risk. As she walked up the porch steps to the huge veranda that circled the Red Thorn Ranch mansion, her legs felt rubbery.

She reminded herself, for at least the hundredth time, that if she lost her chance at the Four C's she could leave this part of Texas. If she took this daring chance and was soundly rejected, it was a shame she wouldn't have to endure long.

She could walk away, find a life somewhere else, someplace where she wasn't known. The world wouldn't care that she was illegitimate or that she'd once been desperate enough to ask a man to marry her. If she failed today, she'd go home and pack her things. There'd be no reason to stay around. After Hank Corbett died, Candice would throw her off the Four C's. Hallie was determined to deny her cousin the pleasure.

The last person Wes Lansing expected to walk into his house was Hallie Corbett. He'd heard old man Corbett was dying but he hadn't felt a speck of sorrow over it.

If his housekeeper had told him it was Candice Corbett waiting in the front parlor, he might have refused to see her. But the news that his visitor was Candy's reclusive cousin Hallie intrigued hell out of him.

Though his sister, Beth, had attended school with Candice and Hallie, he could count on the fingers of one hand the number of times he'd seen Halona . Corbett close up. She hardly ever attended social functions. If she'd ever done anything in her life to attract attention it would have been novel enough to make the papers over half of Texas.

Wes leaned back in the big swivel chair behind his

desk as he waited for his housekeeper to show Hallie to the den. Whatever she wanted couldn't be half as interesting as the fact that she'd come to Red Thorn and asked to see him.

As she followed the housekeeper down the long hall to the den, Hallie gripped the neatly folded copy of the Last Will and Testament of Hank Corbett. The will laid out precisely the conditions of her inheritance. That it required the "husband of Halona Corbett's choice," and didn't specifically prohibit her choosing Wes Lansing, made this last gamble possible.

The housekeeper stopped outside the door and motioned her inside. Hallie stepped over the threshold and felt her courage waver.

Wes sat behind his big desk. The moment she walked in, his eyes met hers with a force that almost made her falter. A wave of terror rolled over her from scalp to toe, sending a sharp charge through her that made her bones shake.

The dark-haired giant behind the desk slowly came to his feet in a gesture of respect that caught her off guard. His dark eyes never left hers. His intensity sharpened and she had to fight not to glance away.

He was searching for something, seeking. Years of enduring her grandfather's relentless search for vulnerability should have made her immune to this. It surprised her to feel so transparent, so threatened.

"Ms. Corbett."

His low voice was as dark as bourbon and hit her insides with as much kick. The strange warmth that started somewhere in the region of her stomach and flowed outward disrupted her even more.

All at once, the painful emotions of the past few hours caught up with her and she struggled to shore up her nerve. If he would just look away from her a moment, allow her to recover, let her catch her breath.

"Thank you for seeing me."

His intensity eased and his strong mouth curved in faint acknowledgment of what they both knew: Corbetts weren't welcome on Red Thorn.

The hint of a smile softened his expression and oddly relaxed her a bit. It suggested that not *every* Corbett was unwelcome, that he'd perhaps withheld judgment in her case.

The moment she registered the impression, she discounted it. The enmity he must surely bear her grandfather and cousin would naturally be conferred on her. She'd be a fool to think otherwise.

Suddenly she was aware that he was sizing her up, that he'd used her momentary distraction to study her. But this time, his gaze dropped from her face and made a slow journey down her work shirt and jeans to her boots. The trip back was much slower.

No man had ever looked at her so thoroughly. Her first impulse was to cover herself, to hide. But she couldn't seem to move. And she couldn't keep from making the same long slow inventory of him.

Wes Lansing was easily over six feet tall. He was built like any other vital man who worked a ranch for a living, but somehow, broad-shouldered, narrow-hipped and well-muscled seemed an inadequate description. For a woman who rarely took note of the male physiques she worked next to each day, she was oddly compelled to note everything about him.

His face fascinated her. Below his dark, overlong hair, his features were rugged and harshly cut, hawkish and primitive. He might have been a homely man if he'd had less presence and if his face hadn't been such a strong indicator of male character. His was a blunt, overpowering masculinity that made her feel fragile and feminine. It was a shocking reaction for a woman who'd rarely allowed herself to consider her femininity or to even think of herself in such precise terms.

Wes took his time. Hallie Corbett was a surprise. She was tall and slender, but she had the right amount of feminine charm in all the right places. Too right, if the heat that surged through his groin was a sign. She had a regal dignity, but there was a faint check in the way she held herself that suggested humility. And yet humility wasn't it.

His gaze returned to her face and he saw the stain of embarrassment on her cheeks. Her long, dark hair was a thick, rich brown, and it was skinned back with a hair tie that smothered whatever lush waves it might have.

But it was her eyes that caught him. Again. They were a rare shade of blue somewhere between warm and cool, but deep, mysterious. And cautious. She was so guarded.

And she was unaware that he felt her unease. She would have hidden it from him if she'd guessed. He sensed that she hid everything. Considering the s.o.b.

who'd raised her, he wasn't surprised.

"You had a reason for coming to Red Thorn?"

His question sent fresh color into her cheeks. She started toward the desk. He noticed she didn't take one of the wing chairs in front of it, but then, he hadn't invited her to sit. It was rude of him, but it was also a test. Corbetts comported themselves as high holies born to rule and reign over lesser mortals.

Hallie Corbett stopped in front of the desk. She held a wad of folded papers in her hand—legal ones, from the look of them—and gripped them as if she thought they'd get away from her. It was plain she wouldn't sit down unless invited.

Her voice was soft, but clear and distinct.

"I came to ask if you're still interested in the parcel of land on the back corner of the Four C's."

Wes was instantly alert. That parcel of land, the site of the original Lansing homestead, had been stolen by the Corbetts in a land swindle and fought over for generations. Blood had been shed on both sides in the ownership dispute. Any number of Corbetts had sworn to never allow a Lansing to reclaim it.

"Is Hank offering it?" Wes was deliberately noncommittal. What interested him now was Hallie's reaction. Had the quick shadow that crossed her face been a show of panic?

"No, sir."

Though he was watching her face closely for a clue about why she'd come here and brought up the subject of the homestead, he saw nothing. Her features were now as blank as uncarved stone.

"Since Hank owns Four C's and he's not offering it, you and I've got nothing to talk about."

Hallie's gaze dropped from his. She unfolded the packet of papers. He sensed that the reason her slim, competent fingers were taking care to flatten the creases in the documents was because she was giving herself time to recover from his rebuff. It was also a delay.

She finished with the task and looked over at him. Her voice was the same clear, even and distinct tone that was evidence of how closely she guarded herself.

"You should have all the facts about ownership before you make that decision. I need to know if you want the parcel."

It was a small showdown. A test of wills. He felt a spark of satisfaction. Hallie Corbett had a backbone behind all that mystery and guarded caution.

"Yes, Ms. Corbett, I'm interested in the parcel. Have a seat and tell me why you think you and I have anything to talk about."

Hallie handed over the papers. She sat down in the chair and braced her elbows on the chair arms. She laced her fingers together and regarded him steadily as he sat down on the swivel chair behind his desk.

"If you'd read the highlighted section…"

Hallie let her voice trail off. She couldn't bring herself to say more. The shame she felt was over-whelming suddenly. Why on earth had she ever thought Wes Lansing would marry her? He wasn't the sort of man who'd ever consider marriage to someone like her, not even to get something he wanted. Unless he valued that land as much as she valued Four C's, he'd find her situation laughable.

And when he laughed, then perhaps ridiculed her, it would be over. She'd withstand whatever he said or did, then make an escape that would be something only a little less dramatic than running away like a scalded dog. She'd go to Four C's, pack her things, then indulge in a last farewell.

It could be over by nightfall. She'd get a room in town until Hank's funeral, then be on her way to a new life far from the shame and pain and loss that were the only legacy she could ever claim here. Her eyes stung and she clenched her teeth together so hard that they hurt, but she'd claw her eyes out before she'd show tears to a Lansing or anyone else.

She focused on Wes's face as he read the section, waiting for the moment he realized what the clause meant and what she was here to suggest.

While she watched his gaze sweep left to right and drop down line by line, she witnessed his stern expression evolve into harshness. She saw the hint of anger in the way the hard line of his mouth tightened. She'd figured him for a second read through, but his dark gaze shot up and arrowed into hers.

"What the hell kind of Will is this?"

She didn't answer because she didn't know what to say. "I'd like to inherit Four C's, but I can't meet the conditions. I thought you should be informed. In case—"

She cut herself off. She couldn't bring herself to actually make the proposal. Suddenly she wanted to be anyplace but here. For once, the shame she was about to earn for herself seemed far more traumatic than losing the Four C's.

"I hope you'll pardon me, Mr. Lansing." She got up and stepped to the desk. "You were right. We have nothing to discuss."

She put out a hand for the papers. "I'll be on my way."

That last came out on a voiceless gust. Emotions she could barely contain came roaring up and it took everything she had to appear indifferent. "If I might have the papers?"

Wes's gaze was riveted to hers, making it impossible to break contact. He ignored her request. "Do you trust Hank to honor this Will?"

Hallie withdrew her hand. He was angry, but it wasn't directed at her. She kept silent as he went on.

"What will you do if he makes another one?"

Hallie fought to keep her gaze locked with his. "I've lived with him all my life, Mr. Lansing. I'm aware of the risk."

"But you came here anyway."

She could tell nothing from his harsh expression, but she didn't detect scorn. And she was a master at that.

"I want Four C's."

"You're crazy to think he'll let you have it."

The words sent a wave of shame through her. Even Hank Corbett's enemies knew how little he thought of her.

"You came here for…what?"

A long moment dragged by as she debated what to say. She couldn't bring herself to tell him outright that she'd come here with a marriage arrangement in mind.

"I couldn't stand by and do nothing."

Wes's hard gaze was unrelenting. "How sick is he?"

"Terminal. He could die tonight or he could live a month. They moved him into Intensive Care late this morning."

"D'you think your cousin would sell me the homestead?"

The question stung. Of course he'd pass over her and go straight to Candice. Perhaps he'd had second thoughts about her cousin. Candice was beautiful, and she'd soon be a fabulously wealthy heiress. The right man might be able to control her and Hallie sensed that if Wes Lansing couldn't do it, it couldn't be done. He might not be as immune to her cousin as she'd thought.

"She doesn't care about Four C's. I expect her to sell it at the first opportunity. You should be able to deal with the new owner."

"But you can't swear she'll sell out."

"You could buy the parcel from her."

His stern mouth twisted. "With strings attached."

"Then you understand Candice."

Wes tossed the Will onto the desk and looked away from her. She started to reach for the papers, but his growl froze her midreach. "Leave 'em."

"I need to be on my way," she said quietly. It wouldn't matter if the copy stayed here. The important thing now was to escape. Wes Lansing was simmering, and she had no desire to watch a boil over.

He glared across the desk at her. "So it comes down to a choice between you and Candice." It wasn't a question. His glare deepened as he nodded toward her chair. "Sit down. You started this, and by God, you'll see it through."

His harshness chilled her. Some faint stir of spirit made her resist. She'd allowed her pride to be trampled by her family all her life. She'd choked on the shreds so she could come to Red Thorn for this last chance. She'd be damned if she let Wes Lansing walk over the battered bits she had left.

"You can keep the Will. Throw it away. Thank you for your time." She turned away from the desk, but she got only two steps before his hard voice stopped her in her tracks.

"You'll not shame me."

The terse words made her glance back at him. "What?"

His dark eyes were fiery and when he slowly stood, she got a frightening impression of power and iron will.

"I won't stand up in front of a justice of the peace with a woman who's dressed like a cowhand."

Hallie turned fully toward him as the shock of what he'd said pounded at her. Surely she'd not heard right.

"We'll fly to Vegas now and be married by tonight." He'd made a decision and issued a decree. And in the spirit of old-time cattle kings, he expected instant obedience.

Maybe he didn't understand the risk. To suddenly capitulate to her unspoken marriage proposal had to mean he didn't take the hazard seriously.

"You were right the first time. Hank will never honor that Will. If he recovers from today's setback and even suspects I've married, he'll call his lawyer and change it. Then you'd be stuck with me."

"I won't be stuck with you. There's always annulment."

The words lashed at her and she fought to keep her voice steady. "By then, you'll have alienated Candice. She'd never take something that once belong—" She cut herself off. "Not that you really would have, but she'd see it that way. She'd never give you a chance at the homestead."

"Too late." His low words sent a shiver through her, and she rushed to make her point.

"Though the Will doesn't prohibit me from marrying you, I think we both know how Hank will take it if he finds out." She looked away from him, unable to bear the conflagration in his dark eyes. "This was a foolish idea. Hank wasn't serious about that Will. He only wrote it to—" she cut herself off, ashamed to reveal the whole truth. "If he lives long enough, he'll change it anyway. It was a huge imposition to bother you. My apologies."

She was so scattered suddenly, so profoundly mortified by what she'd done, that she didn't realize Wes had come around the desk. When his fingers closed around her arm she jumped.

"We can leave for Vegas now. I'll buy whatever you need when we get there."

She looked up at him, searching his granite expression for a clue to such tenacity.

The feel of steely strength in his hard fingers sent a flurry of heat and electricity through her that took her breath away. She'd never felt anything like this, and she was both excited and terrified. She shook her head, so dazed and weak-kneed that she felt faint.

"No—"

"We'll get a lawyer for the prenup. If the old man dies before he can change the will, I want it in writing that you'll sell me the homestead."

She shook her head. "But—I'd give it to you."

"I'll pay cash. Fair market value."

He was implacable. Why had she come to this man? It was true, she'd started this, but she wasn't certain now that she had the courage to finish it. And the biggest reason was Wes Lansing himself. He was too strong for her, too formidable.

"I'm going back to Four C's, Mr. Lansing. Thank you, but this was a mistake."

"We made a decision."

Hallie shook her head. "A decision neither of us can live with. Hank will either die before we can marry or he'll recover and change the will."

"I'm willing to risk it."

"Then we'll both lose."

If it was possible, Wes's features grew more harsh. The hard sparkle in his dark eyes was intimidating. "We could both win. Like I said, you started this. You're gonna see it through."

She tried to pull away from him, but his fingers tightened. He rattled her, excited her and scared her half to death. There was a core reason the Corbetts and Lansings had been at war so many years: they were exactly alike. Hank Corbett was harsh, domineering and unforgiving, and Wes Lansing was cut from the same cloth.

Yet in spite of that, she felt herself respond to him. Instinct told her this was something sexual, something so alien in her experience as a female that she didn't know how to cope with it.

And because she didn't, she suddenly understood why Wes terrified her. He had the power to do what her grandfather hadn't quite managed: Wes Lansing could destroy her. She had to find some way to defend herself, some way to stop this.

"Which means, it's my fault when the bargain goes wrong. No thanks, Lansing."

She almost couldn't bear the sharpness in his gaze as it cut over her face. "I'll take responsibility."

The vow stunned her. She was always blamed. Why should things be different with him? If anything, it would be worse.

"Is that the truth?" She watched temper surge into his dark eyes. But then, she'd just called his honor into question.

His low voice made it clear. "The first thing you need to learn about me is that I mean what I say."

She couldn't tell if he'd meant that as a comfort or a threat.

CHAPTER TWO

THE second thing Hallie learned about Wes Lansing was that he was a despot. Domineering and exacting, with a faint edge of impatience that she sensed more than saw. Before they left Texas, they saw an attorney to draw up the prenuptial agreement that sealed their bargain for the Lansing homestead. They'd also put in writing an agreement that kept either of them from making claim to money or property either of them currently owned or might inherit in the future.

Through it all, Wes seemed to watch every move she made and having so much attention was wearing. She was accustomed to being invisible, so his constant surveillance twisted her nerves so tight that her body felt as taut as piano wire. Her head was pounding by the time their plane touched down in Las Vegas.

In the brisk manner she was quickly coming to expect, Wes ushered her off the jet and through the airport terminal. Unburdened by luggage, they were outside in the Nevada heat far ahead of the swarm of tourists who had packed their flight from Texas. Wes chose the nearest cab and they got in.

Once they'd gotten a marriage license, the afternoon descended into a whirlwind course through the largest shopping mall in Las Vegas. Hours later, they walked out to a waiting cab with the boxes and bags that contained everything Wes decreed was needed for their wedding.

At least she'd paid for her own clothing. Pride dictated it, and a healthy personal bank account made it possible. Neither of them considered the pomp and extravagance of a traditional wedding dress, but she'd ended up buying more than the dress she would wear for the ceremony. Because she owned little more than jeans and work clothes, she took the opportunity to buy three other dresses that appealed to her, along with shoes and lingerie.

Once she'd gone that far, she stopped at a salon where her long hair was shampooed, trimmed, then twisted into a classic style atop her head. She'd even visited a cosmetics counter. Though she'd felt silly letting the clerk talk her into an array of cosmetics, the woman had engineered something of a makeover.

Why had she allowed that?

As Hallie stood in front of the full-length mirror in their hotel suite, she saw her answer in the polished glass.

She no longer looked like a ranch hand; she was a bride. The white linen dress and matching jacket she wore were elegant and sophisticated. The white floppy-brimmed hat that rested stylishly on her upswept hair framed a face that the subtle enhancement of light makeup and lip color had made lovely.

She hadn't known she could look like this. Hadn't suspected. The stifling extreme that kept her every word and act under rigid control had also dictated her secret aversion to adopting any manner or look that could even remotely be interpreted as a challenge to

Candice. It had meant no makeup, no stylish hair-styles, no feminine clothes. She'd smothered almost every natural desire or instinct that might have invited unpleasant comparisons. Or ridicule.

Wes had given her an excuse to indulge her long repressed instincts and she'd gone a little overboard. He now had a bride who wouldn't shame him in front of a justice of the peace, but she could never go back to the Four C's looking like this. After the ceremony, the fine clothing and makeup would come off. Everything she'd bought today would be neatly folded into a box or a bag and the magic would be hidden away in a closet in her bungalow on Four C's. Because it was essential to keep their marriage secret, she doubted anyone but Wes Lansing would ever see her like this. She struggled against the private pain of that.

His bride was a Corbett. He'd kept that fact firmly in mind all afternoon and he'd watched her closely for any sign of perfidy. At first, he'd seen nothing but a reserved, aloof young woman. But the way her gaze frequently shied from his until she rarely looked his way, made him increasingly suspicious. What were her real motives for marriage?

Wes took this moment to study her as he looked through the open door into the suite's bedroom. Unaware of him, Hallie stared into the cheval mirror in the corner. The unguarded play of emotion that crossed her face fascinated him. She searched her reflection as if she'd never seen it before. And maybe she hadn't. He knew instantly that it wasn't conceit that made her stare at herself, it was surprise. The chic female image in the glass bore no trace of the ranch hand he'd left Texas with.

He read her wistful, almost poignant expression and got a fresh glimpse into what her life had been like. Candice Corbett was a spoiled, selfish little witch. The shy, reclusive Hallie probably suffered enough from her cousin without calling attention to the fact that she was beautiful enough to put Candice in the shade if she'd ever half tried.

What kind of female was Halona Corbett? Why would she put up with the mistreatment of her family years past age eighteen when she could have left home and struck out on her own?

He'd seen the passion in her eyes when she'd said she'd not been able to stand by and do nothing to get Four C's, and yet instinct told him she'd stayed for more than a ranch. Could she have been so undermined by her upbringing that she didn't realize that she could go anywhere else and have a better life? Did she have so little self-confidence?

Or did she cling to the ideal of loyalty and duty to family? There was no way to equate family loyalty and duty with her choice to marry into the clan that took up the other side in a generations-long feud. Unless it was part of some new Corbett scheme. Could she be using him in some twisted way to earn her grandfather's approval?

Halona Corbett was a mystery wrapped in an intriguing package. What had started that afternoon as a daring chance to reclaim the homestead had evolved into much more by nightfall. There was no denying that his instant attraction to her had made her offer of a bargain more compelling, and that his vigilance that day had made him even more aware of her as a woman.

In the end, he had to remember that she'd been raised on morals and values that changed to suit selfish whims. She was a woman who'd been taught from the cradle that dishonesty was permitted if it was carried out with cunning and style.

Which was why he'd insisted on the prenuptial agreement that secured the Lansing homestead and prevented her future claim to Red Thorn. If Hallie turned out to be no different than any other Corbett, he'd have something to take into court.

He stepped into the bedroom to get her attention. God help her if she went back on her word.

Hallie caught sight of Wes in the mirror and was ashamed to be caught looking at herself. *Admiring* the way she looked. A hot flush spread up her face to her hairline.

Wes was so ruggedly handsome in his severe black three-piece suit that her breath grew unsteady. He looked powerful and unabashedly male, and she felt a peculiar excitement. Something feminine in her had came to vibrant life and she suddenly craved an acknowledgment from him, some sign of male approval from a man so blatantly masculine that his nearness made her heart race.

Her gaze went to Wes's as if drawn by a magnet. She saw the dark flicker of interest in his eyes, but then it vanished and left her with the sinking feeling that she'd imagined it. To conceal her disappointment, she glanced away from him, self-conscious. She turned from the glass and walked to the dresser where she'd left her handbag. She felt his gaze follow her every move.

Wes's voice was carefully neutral. "Did you call the hospital?"

"Yes," she answered quietly. "There's no change."

"Still want to go through with this?"

The question made her look over at him. She could tell nothing from his solemn expression. "Do you?"

Wes's dark gaze narrowed on her face and she felt herself go tense. He was searching again, seeking. How on earth could she go through with a marriage to this man? She felt no more comfortable in his presence now than when she'd walked into his house that afternoon. Though they would never live under the same roof as man and wife, she wasn't certain she could tolerate the pressure of his occasional presence or the confusion of emotion and sensation he made her feel.

"Some folks will believe you're betraying blood to marry me."

His grim words made her heart fall. The guilt that had nagged her all day suddenly blossomed. She thought of the ranch and what it meant to her, then she thought of her family and the cruel words that had driven her to this.

You've been a shame on this family since your mama brought you home to me, Hank had said. *Bastard's one thing, but I won't let a misfit inherit Four C's.*

Her throat thickened with pain. There were only a

handful of times in her life that her grandfather had ever spoken kindly to her. And those times he'd been manipulating her.

"Wouldn't they believe the same of you?" she asked softly.

"They might. But the difference is, Hank raised you and he's still alive. You owe him for taking you in."

The familiar frustration began to rise. "He took in Candice, too. I don't think you'd ask her about family loyalty."

"I wouldn't have to. Candice is so loyal to Hank that marrying me would be seen as a scheme to get Red Thorn." His gaze suddenly sharpened on her face and his voice went dangerously soft.

"If you have anything else in mind but our bargain, any twisted notion that you're putting me in a situation that Hank can exploit, you need to know that you're the one who'll suffer most. You mean nothing to me. Being my legal wife will matter even less."

Hallie felt something in her heart quiver and shrink in on itself. He meant every word and she had no doubt that he'd be utterly ruthless with her. His judgment would be swift and sweeping. His retaliation would be brutal and calculated to devastate.

She could see that he was already so suspicious of her that one wrong word, one mistaken action could provoke him to act first and check the facts later. She would never think to conspire against him, but how easy would it be for Hank, if he lived long enough to find out, or Candice, to make it look as though she had?

Emotion roared up and sent a stinging fullness into

her eyes. She'd been so desperate to get the ranch that she'd blinded herself to the very personal peril Wes Lansing represented. To have him state it so starkly made her feel foolish and hopelessly naive.

She was standing between two ruthless men who placed no value on her above making her a handy target for their displeasure. And perhaps she deserved it for putting herself in range when she was too powerless to fight either of them and win.

Hallie gripped her handbag, then looked away from him before the telling blur in her eyes could spill over and shame her. She set the handbag on the dresser, then reached up to find the hat pin that secured her hat to the mound of locks arranged so artfully atop her head. She must look as ridiculous and pretentious to him as she felt.

She removed the pin and pulled off the hat. Her fingers were trembling as she pushed the pin into the crown to safely anchor it. She managed to keep her voice clear and steady.

"I'll reimburse you for the plane tickets, the room—everything. If you'll put a dollar value on your time, I'll pay you for that, too. I'd appreciate if you kept this confidential." She paused. "I realize I can't stop you if you choose to make it public."

"So this was a setup." His voice had a deadly edge to it.

Hallie made herself look over at him. His rugged face was the picture of suppressed fury.

"It wasn't. But you've just made me realize how easily *I* could be set up if my family finds out. I've survived my life so far, Mr. Lansing," she said, then leveled what she considered the ultimate insult. "I won't put myself at the mercy of a man no better than my grandfather."

Bad temper blazed in his dark eyes, but Hallie turned away to gently set the stylish hat on the dresser. She held herself with the same stiff dignity that she relied on to maintain her composure, but she wasn't certain it would save her this time. Her insides were boiling with humiliation and her face felt on fire. It didn't help that her legs felt heavy and her knees were weak. She'd lost her chance.

But now that she had, she forced herself to focus on the thought that this was the beginning of her new life. There would be no Hank Corbetts in it and no Wes Lansings. She'd never have Four C's, but she wouldn't have to take the terrible risk of marrying a stranger—a family enemy—to get it.

The moment Wes stepped out of the room, she could close the door and shut him out. She could recover in the privacy and solitude that were so dismally familiar to her. He would leave the suite, but she could stay here. Maybe she'd stay the night. She'd be paying for it. She always paid.

Wes's voice was low and rough. "We're strangers to each other, Miz Corbett."

Hallie glanced warily at him and tried to read his stern expression. His face was far less harsh now, and the dark fire in his eyes had faded.

"If I've misjudged you, I apologize."

She looked at him gravely. "I'm not smart enough or brave enough to be part of any scheme against you that I'm aware of. If my grandfather is manipulating either of us beyond what is obvious in that Will, I'm not a party to it. Nor would I be.''

He stared at her for long moments and again, it seemed as if all the intensity he was capable of was focused on her. Those moments were almost unbearable, but she tolerated them. He was weighing her by her words, measuring what he could see in her to make up his mind. It felt as if he were examining every atom and circuit in her brain.

It was rare to meet someone who mistrusted her almost as deeply as she mistrusted others. Strangely, it made her feel less guarded, less threatened to know that someone as powerful as Wes Lansing thought she might have the potential to injure him somehow. At last, he spoke.

"If we marry, your loyalty belongs to me."

His demand didn't really surprise her, but she felt a prickle of anger. "What about your loyalty, Lansing? Will it belong to me?"

The firm line of his mouth went stern. He must not have expected that. And he didn't appear happy about it, either. He wasn't accustomed to giving an inch to anyone, and it probably rankled to contemplate the notion.

"Because if we marry," she went on, "I think that entitles both of us to equal expectations. If you expect loyalty from me, I expect just as much from you. The fact that the marriage is secret makes no difference."

He gave her a narrow look that hinted he was reassessing her in some way. He confirmed the impression with his next words.

"You're a surprise." His dark gaze released hers

to move slowly down the length of her. The bold stroke sent a warm shiver through her. His gaze returned to hers and she struggled to appear unaffected. "I'm not sure yet if I like it."

Hallie had no reply to that so she kept silent, enduring the tension between them while she fought to withstand it.

"I do like the hat," he said finally. "If you'll marry me, I'd like to see you wear it."

His low words sent a poignant ache through her. However small a remark it was, whether he'd meant it to be or not, it was somehow a validation of the pains she'd taken to look like a bride.

"If you're sure." Her voice had choked to a whisper and she cringed inwardly. She hated that she'd revealed that much.

Wes slipped a finger into the vest pocket of his black suit and stepped toward her. Her breath caught as he reached for her left hand and lifted it between them.

She was so surprised that she almost stepped back, but just that quickly, he lightly singled out her ring finger and slid on a diamond ring. A whirl of sensation spiraled through her. His big fingers tightened gently on her hand as she stared down at it in disbelief.

The diamond sparkled and the gold band it was mounted on caught the suite lights. It fit perfectly.

A huge swell of emotion surged up and left her shaken. She hadn't thought about rings. Theirs wasn't a true marriage where rings were called for to signify unending love and eternal commitment.

"I can't wear this," she whispered. She couldn't wear the beautiful engagement ring, she shouldn't, but she couldn't take her eyes from it. And she couldn't keep her heart from breaking over the gesture. "Please...take it off."

"It's tradition."

"This isn't a real marriage. It's enough of a sacrilege to marry for—for the reasons we are," she got out hastily.

His fingers tightened gently, prompting her to look up at him. "Does it bother you to marry to get a piece of land?"

She couldn't bear the new sharpness in his dark eyes and her gaze fled his as she gave a small nod. She pulled her hand from his and immediately took hold of the ring to take it off. "Of course it bothers me."

He caught her hands before she could remove the ring.

"It'll be public knowledge when he dies and it comes out that you fulfilled the Will's requirements."

Hallie looked up at him urgently. "But he can't find out before he..." Suddenly she couldn't say the word.

Wes's dark brows lowered in disapproval. "I'm not much for secrets. He knows he threw down the gauntlet with that Will. If he lives, how long do you think you can keep your marriage from him? How good an actress will you have to be to quiet his suspicions?" He paused and his voice lowered. "How many lies are you capable of telling to keep him from changing the Will?"

Hallie managed to pull her hands from the steely warmth of his. The tingly heat they generated had added a distressing dimension to his disturbing words.

"Then going through with the marriage is futile."

"We knew that was the risk. We decided to marry because it's worth taking a chance." His stern mouth gentled and one corner turned up in a half smile. "And we came to take our chance in a city known for high-stakes gambling and quick marriages."

Hallie looked away. Everything had seemed so simple hours ago. She'd been so hurt, so angry and torn up over the cruelty of Hank's will that she hadn't completely considered the full consequences of this rash act.

"If Hank lingers and it comes out," he went on, "there are certain marriage traditions I want people to know we observed. Rings are one."

"Everyone will know it wasn't a traditional marriage," she said quietly. "And it will be annulled right away."

She'd have enough to live down over the annulment. She didn't want to give anyone the impression that she'd had any sort of hope for a real future with Wes.

She shook her head. "The ring is too symbolic." Again she started to take off the beautiful ring, but his hands again caught hers.

"Then don't wear it at home," he said sternly. "But you'll wear it here. And the wedding band that goes with it."

Hallie looked up at him, about to protest, but he cut her off.

"It's getting late. If we're going to do this, we've got to get it done. I made plans for ten o'clock, and it's nine-thirty now."

Her throat spasmed closed in alarm. They'd delayed long enough. The longer the delay, the more reservations she had about going through with it. In the end, it was the craving to inherit Four C's that made her force away her growing misgivings and give a small, stiff nod.

"All right."

As if those strangled words were the pistol shot that started a race, her heart burst into a panicked rhythm. Wes stood nearby while she got the hat and pinned it on with fingers that seemed abnormally clumsy. Then he whisked her out of the suite so quickly that he made her head spin.

Did Wes realize he was torturing her?

Hallie had trouble meeting the minister's eyes. She was excruciatingly aware that Wes had not taken her to one of the many wedding chapels in Las Vegas; he'd taken her to a real church, with an ordained minister.

The church was large and a sacred atmosphere permeated every inch of it, including the small prayer chapel they were standing in. This was no secular ceremony before a justice of the peace or one in a commercial chapel where a lineup of brides and grooms waited to be married. This was a real church, and there was no way to ignore the fact that they were pledging vows before God.

She hadn't voiced her objections to Wes. She'd been uneasy when they'd arrived at the church, but as they followed the minister who'd met them at door and led them to the chapel, her unease had increased with each step.

Now the minister had started the ceremony and the significance of what they were doing pressed down on her. Marriage vows were supposed to be a solemn pledge of love and marital commitment, which were as much a vow to God as to each other. She was secretly marrying to secure an inheritance for what amounted to financial gain, and the guilt of that made every word the minister said weigh a thousand pounds.

"And do you, Halona Corbett, take Wes Lansing as your lawfully wedded husband, to love him and care for him, in sickness and in health, as long as you both shall live?"

Her throat closed and she couldn't speak. The silence stretched. The minister waited patiently, his kind eyes regarding her with a gentleness that somehow pierced her guilt and sent a tiny trickle of peace into her heart.

Something hopeful began to make itself felt. It was then that she realized what that hope was: she hoped Wes would find something about her he could love.

For a woman who'd known little love and, until that moment, had no real expectations to find it, she was astonished to realize how deep the craving to love and be loved went. Surely she wasn't foolish enough to open her heart to the possibility of love with a stranger when her own family had found it impossible to love her?

When she finally got out the words, "I do," she realized with secret horror that she wanted to make true every word she'd just pledged, that somehow her heart had staked its survival on the impossible hope that Wes might someday want to honor his vows to her.

Suddenly she was trembling and she felt faint. She couldn't keep from looking up at Wes as the minister read his part of the vows. Wes's dark eyes were somber as he stared down into hers. His voice was a quiet rasp as he said, "I do."

Their gazes clung. The utter seriousness of the vows seemed to have affected them both. Hallie couldn't break contact with his gaze. Her heart beat so swiftly and so hard that she felt it bruise her chest.

The minister's voice was pleasant and cheerful. "I now pronounce you husband and wife. You may kiss your bride, Mr. Lansing."

Hallie heard the words then stared in disbelief as Wes leaned closer and his dark head descended. *He was going to kiss her!* She was too shocked and too mesmerized by the idea to move.

His lips were firm and warm as they settled on hers. She started to jerk back from the contact, but suddenly his hand slipped behind her neck and she couldn't retreat. Panic made her go rigid, but in that next heartbeat of time, the lightning bolt of feeling that went through her turned her bones to mush and her eyes fell shut. If his other hand hadn't slipped around her waist to hold her up, her knees would have given out.

When he withdrew, she opened dazed eyes to see the dark fire in his. Male knowledge blazed arrogantly in their depths, and she knew without a doubt that with one brief kiss, he could tell that not only had she never known a hint of sexual intimacy, she'd also never been kissed. But then she caught a glint of suspicion, as if he suddenly mistrusted her.

It was all she could do to wait for the minister's final blessing and they signed the wedding license. The two female employees from the church office who'd witnessed the ceremony hugged her.

By the time they walked out of the church and down the front steps to a waiting cab, Hallie was queasy and her head was starting to pound.

They ate supper in a quiet restaurant and barely spoke to each other. The mood between them was somber. Hallie was certain she wouldn't be able to eat, but once she had a bite of the tender steak Wes ordered for her, her appetite came back with a vengeance. The meal helped soothe her nerves and her headache vanished. They were leaning back with the wine that he'd insisted they have when Wes spoke.

"I should have called for room service when we first got to the hotel. I didn't mean to make you wait so late to eat."

Hallie looked over at him. The apology warmed her and made her feel as if he cared for her at least a little. But it was dangerous to think that way.

His gaze dropped to her lips and the flash of intensity in his dark eyes reminded her of the kiss in the chapel. Longing gripped her and she glanced down at her wineglass to hide it.

Would she ever have a chance to feel the expert pressure of his lips on hers again, to feel that heat, to be caught in the wild, sweet storm of feeling that had gone through her?

Something wounded in her warned that she'd had her taste, that she was only allotted one; but the part of her that was unbearably lonely and lost craved another chance and refused to stop hoping.

To her utter humiliation, her thoughts must have shown, because Wes remarked, "I didn't intend for the ceremony to seem so…binding. But the other kind didn't seem right."

There it was. The admission that the church ceremony had given an impression he hadn't intended. The foolish little hope that had made itself felt in the chapel died a swift death. She quickly finished her wine and made herself look over at him.

"Would you…mind?" She pushed the wineglass toward him and he obliged her by refilling it. She had another glass before they left the restaurant to go back to their hotel.

The cab ride was silent. Hallie took off the hat and leaned her head back against the seat to quietly watch the millions of casino lights glitter and flash past her window. The wine had relaxed her, but she felt more subdued than usual.

The sidewalks were crowded with gamblers and vacationers eager for the nightlife of Las Vegas. The whole town was light and energy and excitement, but none of it touched her.

If the circumstances of their visit hadn't been so serious, she might have enjoyed going into a casino, maybe trying her luck at a game of chance, to at least see what the attraction was. But the knowledge that she'd just married a man to get a ranch, and that, in essence, she was betting her grandfather would die before he found out, made her feel heartless and mercenary.

It didn't matter to her conscience that Hank had barely tolerated her, that there were times when he'd been unbearably cruel. He was her grandfather. Whether that had ever meant anything to him or not, it had meant something to her. Which was why his treatment of her all these years had so wounded her, and had possibly influenced this disloyal act.

They arrived back at their hotel. Wes paid the driver and they got out to walk into the hotel and cross the lobby to the elevators. When one arrived, they stood aside as the passengers got off.

The last three passengers who stepped out were older women. One of them glanced at Wes and gave a startled look.

"Why, Wes Lansing. What a surprise! And—" she looked at Hallie with great interest "—who's this lovely young woman?"

In the next second, the woman's gaze dropped to the hat that Hallie carried in her left hand, and her face showed fresh surprise as she eyed the rings.

"My goodness, Wes, is this your bride?"

CHAPTER THREE

HALLIE stood next to Wes as the elevator glided upward. She fidgeted with the hat, so distressed she could barely stand still. Because they were alone, Wes spoke.

"Edna Murray is the biggest gossip in our part of Texas. She might not wait to get home to report this."

Hallie felt sick. Edna Murray was her punishment for taking vows in church that she knew she'd have to break. Now there was no hope of keeping their marriage secret until her grandfather passed away. Edna's almost giddy, *So, this is the end of the feud—how romantic!* haunted her.

The moment they reached their floor and the doors opened, Hallie rushed out. She got to their room several steps ahead of Wes, then had to wait for him to open the door. When he did, she started to go in, but he caught her arm. Her gaze flew to his.

"Just a minute."

Before she realized what he intended, he leaned toward her, then swept her off her feet into his arms. She immediately tried to wiggle out of his hold.

Though Hallie was strong for her lithe size, Wes's easy strength made her feel fragile when he flexed his arms and held her firmly. He carried her over the threshold into their suite, then set her on her feet.

Hallie stepped away from him as if she'd been burned.

"Why did you do that?" She couldn't take her eyes from his stern expression as she searched it for a clue to why he'd carried her in.

"Now that we can't hope to keep this marriage secret, we need to think about observing the traditions people expect."

Hallie shook her head. "No one could have seen what you just did."

Wes walked to the cabinet that concealed a small bar and opened the door. "They'll see whether or not we live together on Red Thorn."

Hallie stared as a new horror presented itself. "I can't live with you."

He glanced her way and his dark gaze went over her from head to foot before returning to her face.

"How much pride have you got, Mrs. Lansing?

He looked back to the cabinet and began to twist open the caps of four small bottles of whiskey, which he divided into two stout tumblers as he went on.

"Now that we've been found out, do you want people to know this was a cold-blooded marriage of convenience to thwart your grandfather? Or would you rather they think it's an impetuous marriage that somewhere down the line doesn't work out?"

Hallie stood stiffly as she stared at him in shock. He picked up the tumblers and carried them to her. She set her hat and handbag on the sofa table, then took the glass he pressed into her shaking hand.

"Maybe you should sit down before you drink that."

She ignored the suggestion and hastily had a sip, then choked on the stinging liquid. Wes calmly watched her and had a taste of his own.

"If Hank doesn't last long enough to find out, I vote for letting people think what they choose, since we'll both have what we married to get. That'll come out right away when the will is read. Most folks have a poor opinion of Hank Corbett. When they find out about what he did to you with that Will, they'll understand."

Hallie's voice was still raspy from the harsh liquor. "And if he lives long enough to find out?"

"Then, since he'd probably write you out of the will completely, I favor the look of a real marriage."

Her quiet, "So that's why you asked about pride," was barely audible. The way she said the word was no endorsement of it.

"I'm not eager to be seen as a man who married a woman to get land, then cast her off the moment he found out she couldn't give it to him. So we'll give the look of a real marriage. Starting now."

"Maybe I don't care what people think." She had another quick sip of whiskey. It didn't sting so much this time.

"I think you do care, A lot. Why else have you kept yourself hidden away on Four C's all this time if you weren't afraid to find out what people think of you? And then there's your charming cousin Candice."

His perception was painful, and she turned away with her drink. She was so rattled that she downed the rest of the whiskey and stood gripping the glass in both hands. "What makes you think you know so much?"

"Because if it wasn't true, you'd tell me so straight out. Instead, you challenged me."

The impression she got—that he could read her mind—made her feel exposed and vulnerable. At first, she thought it was panic that made her suddenly feel dizzy. But in the next second, she realized that the whiskey she'd downed so fast was already making itself felt.

"I'm afraid...of a lot of things," she found herself admitting.

The terrible craving to let someone know her—the hope that she might reveal herself to another person and be liked—was suddenly close to the surface. And it was stronger with Wes than with anyone she'd ever met in her life. It terrified her to wonder what that meant.

The memory of the somber little ceremony in the chapel came back to her. Something had happened when she'd made that vow. Somehow, some way, her heart had reached for something it needed and grabbed on hard.

"I've made a terrible mistake." Her voice trembled on the word. She'd not only lost her chance, she'd exposed the needs and desires and desperate hopes that she'd hidden from herself and everyone else all her life. These few hours with Wes had done that, and she was suddenly overwhelmed by it all.

The next thing she knew, Wes had moved beside her and was taking the empty glass from her hands.

He set it on the sofa table along with his own. He took her arm and started to lead her to a chair.

"You need to sit down."

The warm sensuality that bloomed at his touch spread through her like syrup. She pulled away, but stepped wrong on the narrow heel of her shoe and faltered. Wes caught her arm to steady her. She braced a hand on his chest, then jerked it away, dismayed by the hard warmth beneath her palm.

"I need to go to bed," she got out, but when she tried to pull from him again, another bout of dizziness made her awkward.

"Maybe you do." And then he was leading her to her bedroom, his easy strength leaving her no choice but to let him have his way.

She managed to pull free once they were in the bedroom and he got her to the bed. She was so anxious to escape his warm grip—to escape her reaction to it—that she took a wary step away. The edge of the mattress brushed the backs of her legs and brought her to a halt.

"You can sleep alone tonight," he said, "but that'll have to change when we get back to Texas."

"I don't like that you're…taking over." The words came out in an uneven rush. Her eyes felt abnormally round as she looked up into his stern expression to watch for any signal that he might touch her again. His dark gaze narrowed on her.

"You don't like it when I take over, but you hate it when I touch you. Why is that?"

She barely had time to recover from the blunt question before his voice went low. "Is it sexual inexperience, or do you find me repulsive?"

Her head spun from the surprise of that. She briefly lifted trembling fingers to her temple.

"And if you find me repulsive, is it because I'm a Lansing?" He studied her face with cold speculation. "Maybe big, rough-looking men aren't your type. You like the handsome ones?"

That was the question that truly stunned her and she struggled to clear the fuzziness from her brain. It was an amazing chink of vulnerability in a man she'd decided had no vulnerabilities.

"You don't like to look at me, you go stiff as a fence post when I touch you, and your lips were sealed so tight when I kissed you that dynamite couldn't have blown them apart. That's either inexperience or revulsion. Maybe both."

His hard expression made her queasy. She could see him close his mind to her, see him judging her a shallow, worthless female. But it was the hint of vulnerability that made her feel a tenuous connection to him, that compelled her to reveal something about herself that she never would have otherwise.

She impulsively reached to touch him before she caught herself and froze with her fingers a mere inch from his hard chest. Nevertheless, she felt his heat radiating through his shirt and vest. His hand came up and caught hers as if to prevent her from touching him. She watched his dark expression, unable to keep from feeling terrified. But whether it was terror of him or terror of herself, she realized she couldn't apportion it that precisely. Her mouth went dry.

"You..." Her voice choked to a whisper. "You're right. I'm not...experienced. At all. And when you...touch me, I worry about what I feel." She had to stop. She swallowed hard and her gaze fled the harshness in his.

His fingers tightened on her hand. She managed to get a full breath, but it came back out on a gust of nerves she couldn't help. "I— It's not...revulsion."

Silence roared in the wake of her halting explanation. She couldn't bear to look up into his face to see his reaction. She'd just defied the self-protective instincts of a lifetime to explain behavior that must have offended him.

Perhaps he'd found her lack of experience and her awkward confession amusing. Would he laugh? She'd be devastated if he did, but she didn't know how to prevent it. At least he'd understand that sharing his bed was out of the question.

"Look at me, Hallie."

The soft command was gravelly and low. She suddenly realized that he'd placed her hand on his chest and he was holding it there. She felt the steady beat of his heart and felt hers beat at least twice for every pulse of his. She finally dared to look up at him, fighting the swirling sensuality that made her muscles weak and her legs unsteady.

His dark eyes had gone nearly black, and he was focused on her flushed face with an intensity that made her feel bruised. There was no evidence of his reaction to her confession in the stony set of his rugged features and her heart shook with dread.

Until his other arm slipped around her and his head

made a slow descent. She could only watch, trying to read any sign of his thoughts from his hard expression.

His breath touched her face and her lashes dropped shut, as much to brace herself for the kiss as to shut out the confusing glimpse of fierceness in him.

And then his lips feathered onto hers, warm, gentle and careful. She couldn't help her rigidity. She was painfully self-conscious. Were her lips dry enough? How should she kiss him back? Should she put her arms around him?

She felt the shame of her ignorance as those excruciating seconds passed. Wes wanted to kiss her—he *was* kissing her. But she knew instinctively that she was disappointing him. When his mouth eased away from hers, she was certain of it.

His voice was a rough whisper that gusted lightly against her lips. "Don't grit your teeth, let your mouth relax."

A wild spear of excitement went through her. She had no time to prepare before his mouth settled softly on hers a second time.

This time, he expertly parted her lips and she felt the damp stroke of his tongue. Surprise made her draw back, but he followed. Suddenly, his arms went tight around her and his lips took complete possession of hers.

Just that quickly, she caught on to the sensuality of his mouth. She couldn't keep her hands from sliding up his chest and her arms from winding around his neck. The shocking intrusion of his tongue sent a hot lava of weakness through her.

The deep, lazily erotic kiss was both torment and tutor. By the time Wes slowly brought it to an end much later, she felt a peculiar prickle of tears. How had she lived her adult life without this? If she'd known what she was missing, she couldn't have endured it.

And how had she lived without this feeling of closeness, this taste of intimacy? A feeling and taste she'd never felt before and only had now because of Wes's lavish kiss?

As she opened eyelids still weighted by sensual paralysis, she tried to focus on Wes's face. Why had he done this? What had this kiss meant?

His voice was gruff, but she caught the steely edge to it. "If this is gonna look like a real marriage, you can't shy away from me like I'm some stranger."

Disappointment swept her. The kiss had been the equivalent of an icebreaker, meant to loosen her up. It had never been meant as an expression of attraction.

She'd trusted him enough to allow it and that amazed her almost as much as his real reason for kissing her hurt her feelings. She lowered her hands to his chest and tried to ease away, but managed only scant inches of space before the world began to shift and her head went foggier. She should never have had the whiskey. Wes steadied her.

"Whoa there. You need help to get ready for bed?"

Now his voice held a touch of soft amusement, but she suddenly didn't care. He could laugh all he wanted because she deserved it. She'd lost her mind over the chance to inherit Four C's. This whole day was her punishment for being so foolish.

"Please leave."

Even she could detect the faint slur of her words. Wes slowly released her and she stepped around him to walk carefully across the room. She closed herself in the bathroom and moved unsteadily toward the sink for support. The task of taking off her makeup and brushing her teeth seemed monumental.

Hallie lifted her head and caught sight of her dazed expression in the mirror. Something significant was happening to her, and she was so disoriented by the whiskey that she had no defense against the overwhelming mixture of anxiety and fresh pain that gripped her heart.

She lifted shaking fingers to her lips. The hot sensation of Wes's kiss still scorched them and the phantom taste of his mouth lingered despite the taste of the whiskey.

That next morning, she was awakened by a dull headache. Her body felt as if it was weighted by cement as she struggled to get out of bed. She knew the moment she glimpsed the sunlight that peeked along the edge of the drapes that she'd overslept.

She hurried to the bathroom for a quick shower, then put on the jeans and shirt she'd worn from Texas the day before. The clock on the night table read nine o'clock by the time she got her purchases from the mall organized for the flight home.

Home. The word panicked her. That was the moment she realized that the feelings she most associated

with her home on Four C's were pain and excruciating loneliness. Because she'd rarely been farther
from the ranch than town or away from it longer than
a handful of hours, she'd never had an opportunity
for such clarity.

But then, she'd done more than go a few miles
away for a few hours. She'd married Wes Lansing.
Panic surged. In her desperate bid to get Four C's,
she'd probably doomed her chance to get it. And if
she had, then the word home and every feeling she
associated with that word was suddenly overwhelmed
by the sharp fear that her home—whatever it meant
to her—no longer existed.

Wes had waited to order breakfast until he'd heard
Hallie moving around in her bedroom. He'd been up
early and slipped out to buy a couple pieces of luggage to take their purchases on the plane.

He hadn't seriously expected Hallie to be wearing
one of the dresses she'd bought the day before, but
he felt a pinprick of disappointment when she stepped
out of her bedroom wearing her ranch clothes. The
fact that she'd left her dark hair loose to let it ripple
past her shoulders to her waist was a consolation. She
was naturally beautiful, but her apparent ignorance of
that fact intrigued and pleased him. As kissing her
had pleased him.

Hallie felt the bold sweep of Wes's dark gaze like
a touch and avoided it. Thankfully, her handbag and
hat were still on the sofa table, so she had something
to focus on. The need to switch her things from the

new handbag into her old one gave her an excuse to escape him.

"I bought you a suitcase for the plane."

The sound of Wes's voice in the stillness twisted her nerves tighter. Her soft, "Thank you. What time does our flight leave?" got a quick response: noon.

She got her hat and handbag, picked up the suitcase and retreated to her room. She was packed in moments.

When she carried the suitcase out, Wes was just opening the door for room service. She set the case down and waited while a cart was trundled in and their meal was laid out on the table near the windows. When the server finished and left the suite, Wes glanced over at her.

"A good meal and a dose of aspirin might help that headache."

Hallie felt her face warm as she joined him at the table and they sat down. A new bottle of aspirin sat on her side of the table and she reached hesitantly for it. Her gaze touched his.

"Thank you."

Their meal passed in a silence that made her every bite of food hard to swallow. Halfway through her plate of bacon, eggs, hash browns and toast, she gave up and set her fork down. She reached for the coffeepot to pour a second cup for them both.

Wes's gruff thanks drew her gaze to his face and she was relieved he wasn't looking at her. She took the opportunity to study him for a clue to his mood, but his expression was impossible to read.

His dark gaze suddenly came up and locked with hers. "Feeling better?"

"Some."

"Have you talked to the hospital?"

Hallie couldn't maintain contact with the searching intensity of his gaze and glanced down at her cup. "Not yet."

She caught the movement when he set his fork down and sat back with his coffee.

"We'll be in close quarters from now on. You need to get used to me." The soft rasp of his voice touched her in a peculiar way. "Neither one of us will ever be comfortable if you can't relax."

Hallie made herself look over at him. His eyes were so dark, his gaze so piercing. But to her relief, she caught sight of something soft and kind in those dark depths. She couldn't account for the strong emotion that welled up and gave her eyes a quick sting.

"I'm not sure I can." The confession was difficult and came out sounding strained.

"If it's not because I'm a Lansing, then is it because you're afraid of me?"

Hallie felt her throat tighten. "I'm...not comfortable with many people."

"Do you want to be comfortable with me?"

The quiet question fell hard between them. The memory of his kiss the night before, the memory of the vows they'd taken in the church, sent such a longing through her that she felt literal pain.

"I— Is it important to you?" The small stutter sent of flash of heat to her face.

"That depends."

Hallie's gaze fled his. He was pressing her again, pushing at her to reveal herself without giving even a hint of how he wanted her to answer. Or how he would react when she did. Her fingers were wrapped so tightly around her coffee cup that they began to feel numb.

"I'm not certain I know...." Her choked voice trailed off.

"How to answer?" he supplied grimly.

The silence that followed was brief.

"Why don't you try the truth?"

His question shamed her. She rarely revealed her true thoughts and feelings, and usually evaded direct questions. She knew her evasions were a kind of lie, so she often avoided that by keeping silent altogether. Ironically, she'd probably revealed more of her true thoughts and feelings to Wes than she had to anyone. But it wasn't enough for him. He seemed determined to refuse both evasions and silence.

"What's the truth, Halona Lansing? Do you want to be comfortable with me or not?"

Now she caught the thread of impatience in his voice and she knew she was frustrating him. *Disappointing* him. The part of her that had always craved approval and rarely got it was injured by the hint that something in her character disappointed him.

"Yes." She didn't realize she'd said the word aloud until she heard it and tasted the metallic tang of fear on her tongue. She couldn't keep her gaze from lifting to his. A huge tremor went through her. "But I'm not certain it's possible."

The moments ticked by in an eerie slow motion

that made her feel light-headed. His harsh expression didn't change by so much as a flicker.

"Maybe not." The terse words signaled the end of the discussion.

Hallie was on edge the whole flight back to Texas. She'd called the hospital and there'd been no change in Hank's condition.

Wes had insisted on giving the look of a true marriage. Whether Hank recovered and changed the Will, or succumbed before he could, she and Wes would live a public marriage for as long as they agreed was necessary. Now that they were back in Texas, they'd make a brief trip to the hospital. Afterward, Wes would drive her to Four C's for most of her belongings, then she'd move into his house on Red Thorn. She didn't want to dwell on the thought that Wes meant for them to share his bed.

She couldn't let herself think that the move to Red Thorn signaled the permanent loss of her home on Four C's. Besides, she planned to continue working the ranch as she always had. Since she put in long days, that meant she'd only be sleeping at Red Thorn, which would limit her contact with everyone there but Wes. And if her grandfather's health continued to deteriorate, that might mean she'd spend no more than a handful of nights on Red Thorn, perhaps only hours.

The quick visit to the hospital was uneventful. Hank hadn't regained consciousness since his admission to Intensive Care the morning before, and Candice wasn't there visiting.

As they drove down the Four C's ranch drive,

Hallie's anxiety mounted. One of the nurses at the hospital had given them her best wishes on their marriage. Since the news was already known by the hospital staff, Candice had to know.

They'd almost reached the section of the ranch drive that angled toward the main house when Hallie spoke up. "Take the left fork." She caught Wes's questioning glance in her peripheral vision and added, "I don't live at the main house."

Wes didn't remark until he pulled his car to a stop in front of her bungalow. The small, four-room house was in good repair, but compared to the opulence of the main house, it was modest and clearly had been built many years ago to house hired hands.

"How long have you lived here?"

Hallie made herself glance over at Wes as he switched off the engine. She gave him a tense smile. "Have you ever been on Four C's?"

His gaze searched hers. "As far as Corbetts know, never." His stern expression relaxed into the suggestion of a smile. "You think Four C's men will come riding up and throw me off?"

Hallie shook her head. "Twenty years ago maybe."

Wes's voice lowered. "You didn't answer my question."

"Does it matter?" Hallie looked away.

"You're my wife."

She felt a chill gust over her heart. "I don't appreciate manipulation." She'd reached to open her door when Wes caught her wrist.

"Explain that."

Hallie turned back to him. "Saying 'You're my wife' suggests that it means something to you in a way that it doesn't."

"Why can't you tell me how long you've lived in this house?"

His persistence frustrated her. She took a shallow breath. "Maybe I'd rather you didn't know that I've lived in this house for ten years."

His gaze narrowed on her flushed face. "You're what, twenty-three?"

"Almost." She pulled away from him to open her door and get out. She walked briskly to the front porch of the small house, her heart in fresh turmoil. She waited until they were both inside and the door was closed before she turned to him.

"I've changed my mind. I think it would be better if I stay on Four C's after all."

Wes thumbed back his Stetson and looked down at her.

"Why is that?"

Hallie couldn't bear the sharpness in his gaze and glanced away. "Everything's become...complicated. I've decided I don't care what people think. We married for the reasons we did. That's all."

"Are you so terrified to share a small part of someone's life, to share a little of your own?"

The quiet question hit her with surprising force, spearing deep into painful places and stirring an anger she rarely acknowledged. It was a struggle to look at him as if she felt nothing, but she managed it.

"The more someone knows about you, the more power it gives them."

"Power to do what?"

Panic rose up to mix with the anger and frustration she felt. "Whatever their conscience allows."

His gaze narrowed on her face. "You must have me confused with someone else."

His voice was soft but carried an edge that let her know she'd offended him. She hadn't intended that. She *had* intended to keep him at a distance, but she couldn't seem to do it.

Hallie turned and took a few steps away. "I don't know you."

"You think you do," he went on calmly. "The problem is, you think I'm another Hank Corbett."

He made her feel transparent, but his persistence made her feel trapped. "Why do you push me?"

His voice dropped to a soft rasp. "Because you won't let me draw you out."

Hallie fought against the appeal of the way he'd said that, as if he was hinting that he wanted to know her because there might be something about her he liked. Common sense warned that her impression was wrong.

"There's no reason for us to know much about each other."

"You're my legal wife," he said, his voice going stern. "I expect a lot from you, but I'm prepared to give you a lot. Trust to start with. Confidentiality. Which means you can trust me with things like the fact that you've lived in this house since you were twelve or thirteen. Alone, I'm guessing."

Hallie wrapped her arms around her middle, as if to protect herself from the gentle assault of his words.

"And because you're my legal wife and your actions affect me," he went on, "I'm not shy about giving advice or insisting that you take it. So you'll live with me on Red Thorn. We made a bargain and we'll see it through, however it turns out."

Another tremor went through her. *We'll see it through.* She'd faced the darkest times of her life alone and she'd survived them, alone. The mere suggestion that someone was willing to face something difficult with her was both tantalizing and terrifying. Because the offer had come from Wes, it was even more emotionally volatile.

But she sensed a kindness behind his rugged exterior, something compassionate and humane and decent. It surprised her to realize that she already trusted him in more ways than she understood.

The sudden craving to share something with him, however much or little it was, however briefly it lasted, compelled her to give in to his edict, to go with him to Red Thorn. And though she didn't seriously think anything could come of this, it would provide her a step away from Four C's so losing it, when she did, might not be as devastating.

Her soft, "All right," was all she could say without betraying the emotions she could barely control.

Wes's calm, "Pick out what you want to take this trip and I'll start carrying things to the car," helped settle her.

They'd finished collecting most of her things, including her box of legal papers and records, when Candice sent a ranch hand to summon them to the main house.

CHAPTER FOUR

THE Corbett ranch mansion was huge, its two-story, pillared front reminiscent of a southern plantation. The roof shaded a deep stone veranda that boasted planters and hanging pots bursting with flowers. Delicately scrolled wrought-iron furniture gave an impression of wealth, but the hospitality it suggested was little more than window dressing.

As Hallie and Wes stepped onto the veranda and walked to the table where Candice sat, Wes rested his hand possessively on the back of her waist. The chaos his touch set off was muted by the rare sense of security it gave her. Any confrontation she'd ever had with her family, she'd faced alone. The novel sense that someone now stood with her was one that cranked her turbulent emotions higher. She couldn't allow herself to depend on Wes.

Candice sat on a chair next to a glass-topped table, presiding over a frosty pitcher of lemonade and three tall crystal glasses filled with shaped ice cubes. She was wearing a short, white sundress that showed off her golden tan and drew attention to her long, elegant legs. With her salon-tousled blond hair, flawless skin and large, jewel-blue eyes, she looked like an angel who'd floated to earth to dazzle mortals with a glimpse of Heaven. But the haughty lift of her chin and the venomous gleam that made her eyes snap with blue flames were a sure indication of evil.

Hallie made no move to seat herself at the table and Wes followed her lead. She welcomed the impression of ease and power he radiated as he loomed at her side. Candice took note and gave them a saccharine smile.

"Well, well, cousin. You caught yourself a beau."

Candice's gaze flicked from Hallie to Wes. Her smile sparkled with brittle charm as she took a long moment to let her gaze stray over Wes with open appreciation.

"Congratulations, Wesley. Let me be the first to welcome you to the family." She gave a meaningful pause. "I regret I can't invite you two inside, but Halona has a peculiar aversion to going in when our granddaddy isn't at home. Isn't that odd? You'll have to ask her about that sometime."

Hallie's nerves spiked high. It took everything she had to appear unaffected. "Was there something you wanted?"

Candice's beautiful eyes returned to Hallie and she gave a cool smile. "No, cousin. I got what I wanted. Do you think you will?"

Hallie forced a tight smile. "It's not up to me."

Candice's light brow arched high. "No, darlin', it's not." Her smile had lost some of its bright curve. "I was about to offer you something cool to drink, but it's obvious you two lovebirds can't wait to be alone."

Her narrowed gaze took note of the color that rose in Hallie's cheeks, and she glanced speculatively at

Wes. Her smile turned flirtatious. "Isn't it sweet that Hallie saved herself for you? What a treat she must be for an eager bridegroom."

Wes's stony expression didn't change, but Hallie read the chill in his dark eyes. His low, "Afternoon, Miz Candice," was flat with dislike.

Candice showed a flash of discomfort that she quickly masked as she came to her feet. Wes touched Hallie's arm, then eased back to let her cross in front of him to walk to the steps. He followed, then walked at her side to the car, his hand once again resting on the back of her waist.

Neither of them looked back when Candice called out, "Good afternoon, Wesley. I hope to see more of you now that you're a member of the family."

Wes had driven them down the ranch drive and pulled out onto the highway before he spoke.

"I don't want you to be alone with her."

Hallie had been secretly keeping track of his harsh profile. He was deeply angry, but the sense she had— that he was angry on her behalf—was a relief.

"She got in a few digs and tried to cause a problem between us. She'll be satisfied with that until she thinks of something else."

"How long will that take?"

"Candice is very bright and very angry. But Hank's condition is a distraction. It's only worth so much to get at me."

Wes appeared to be thinking that over, so she faced forward and said calmly, "I plan to continue working on Four C's. Candice rarely goes further than the main house when she's at the ranch, so I'll never see her.''

The silence in the car was thunderous. She dared a quick glance at Wes, but his granite profile was harsh. His terse, ''We'll discuss this later,'' signaled his strong objection. The fact that he really didn't plan to discuss anything was clear in the hard flex of his jaw.

She'd been in the Red Thorn ranch mansion for the first time the day before, but she'd seen only a small part. She'd been in such distress that she hadn't noticed many details inside or out. As they pulled up in the part of the drive that curved in front of the huge house, Hallie looked more closely.

The white, two-story Victorian with the wood-railed veranda circling the main floor gave an impression of family and welcome that the main house on Four C's never had.

The potted flowers that dotted this veranda were sturdy and colorful, but not profuse. The patio furniture was whitewashed wood with floral cushions, selected more for function and comfort than to signal wealth or pretense.

Wes told her he'd have someone take her things into the house, so they got out and walked to the front steps. He took her on a quick tour of the main floor of the house, making time to properly introduce her as his wife to his cook, Dora, and his housekeeper, Marie. Both women were delighted at the news of Wes's marriage, but their enthusiastic congratulations and best wishes made Hallie feel guilty.

After that, Wes led her out the patio door off the

kitchen to give her a tour of the headquarters. They ended up at the stables where they saddled two horses and Wes expanded their tour to the land. It was clear he'd had a destination in mind when they arrived at a wide, sandy bank along a shallow creek lined with trees. They dismounted and left their horses to graze on a grassy section of shaded bank, then walked to the water's edge.

The soft sound of moving water was calming. Wes stopped beside her and took off his Stetson to comb his big fingers through his hair before he put the hat back on. Hallie glanced at his rugged profile. The sense she had—that something big was coming—unsettled her. The quiet drawl of Wes's deep voice was soothing, but his words were not.

"We've got some decisions to make." He turned his head and looked down at her. "You aren't gonna work Four C's."

Hallie had known he would object, but this was an order. "You said *we'd* make the decisions," she reminded him stiffly. "What you really meant was that *you'd* make them."

"Cousin Candice is lying in wait for you," he pointed out grimly. "There isn't a man on Four C's who can afford to take your side in any trouble she stirs up."

"I don't expect them to. Nor would I allow it."

The intensity in his dark gaze became more turbulent. "You underestimate the jealousy she feels for you. Every time you go near her from here on, you'll be a target."

Nettled, Hallie looked away and focused on the far

side creek bank. "I don't recall that our bargain included making you either my boss or my protector."

"Think of it as an unexpected bonus. Your independence ended . in that chapel last night, Mrs.
Lansing, and so did mine."

Hallie looked at him in disbelief. He was taking
over. Part of her was angry, yet part of her felt oddly
relieved. It was the part of her that felt relief that she
had to fight. She was too vulnerable to let herself be
fooled into thinking Wes's urge to protect her meant
anything significant.

"You're giving me another version of the 'you're
my legal wife' line," she said quietly. "Only this
time, it's because what I do or what might be done
to me might reflect poorly on your good name."

He gave her a hard look. "You're about half right.
What you do and what might be done to you is something I'll take personally because you're my wife. It
would reflect poorly on me if I allowed upset or harm
to come to my wife because I didn't look out for her
best interests."

His gaze narrowed speculatively on her tense expression. "I'll bet you could prove my point," he
said, then zeroed in. "You've lived alone since you
were twelve or thirteen when, as a member of the
family and an orphaned minor child, you should have
lived at the main house. And according to Candice,
you don't set foot in that house today unless Hank's
there. Explain why."

Old shame seeped into her heart. Her hope that
Candice's remark hadn't made a lasting impression
on him vanished. She should have known better. Wes

missed nothing. She looked away and her teeth clenched together so hard her jaw ached. If she explained, she'd more than prove his point about what Candice was capable of.

Even worse, Candice would never have brought it up if she'd thought there was a chance that Wes would believe Hallie's side of the story.

Wes's voice went low, but the demanding edge was gone. "Candice made my sister's life hell for a couple of years and she was a kid then."

Just when Hallie thought he'd eased up on her, that he no longer expected an explanation, he added, "When you came to me yesterday, you pulled me into Corbett business. I deserve to have answers when I ask for them."

If she'd ever dreamed that she and Wes would have to become so involved that she'd have to tell him anything about her real life, she never would have gone to him. But he was right. She'd got him into this and he deserved answers. Her resentment faded, but the queasiness she felt increased. She couldn't look at him, and her voice sounded as strangled as it felt.

"Hank's sister visited one time and had the bad manners to tell Hank that I was a sweet, mistreated child, but that Candice was a brat who needed counseling. Candice set out to prove I was the bad seed." Hallie paused and tried to swallow away the tightness in her throat. "Someone took scissors to her closet of dresses and her doll collection, and someone 'stole' her favorite necklace, which was later found taped behind my dresser mirror. The scissors were found under my mattress. A maid who saw Candice in my room with the necklace was fired for standing up for me.''

She went silent then and Wes asked, ''Did Hank know the truth?''

''I think he did. Candice got the sheriff involved but he'd figured out what was going on. He threatened to have a social worker intervene on my behalf. Which was why Hank allowed me to move to the other house.''

''Allowed? Or forced?''

''Allowed. I'd been asking since before Candice did that.''

Hallie's insides were twisting with uncertainty. Did Wes believe her? He only had her word for what had happened, and there was no way to prove it now, since the old sheriff had retired years ago.

The curiosity in his voice hinted that he'd believed her. ''Why would you stay on all this time? You could have left Four C's the day you turned eighteen.''

Anger surged, and the strong will that had got her through her life this far made itself felt. ''Because Candice Corbett got everything else that was important to me. Until I know for sure that she gets this, too, she can't run me off.''

Wes didn't comment on that right away, so Hallie's anger had time to cool. Eventually, the soothing sound of the creek began to make an impression, and she became aware that several minutes had passed. She thought the subject was closed when Wes spoke.

"I admire your tenacity, but what are your plans if things don't work out?"

There was a kindness in his tone, something that softened the pang his question caused her. She took a steadying breath and tried to sound unemotional as she blindly stared at the far side creek bank.

"I won't live here, after. I've saved some money and Hank's sister left me a little when she died. It should be enough to get me somewhere and cover things until I find work."

"You know anybody out there in the real world?"

The question nicked her pride, but in light of what he knew about her, it was reasonable.

"I know names."

"Could you run a ranch?"

"I can run Four C's. Anyplace else, I'll be glad to do ranch work." She couldn't imagine doing anything else, but she was practical enough to know she might have to.

"Hired hands don't get rich."

"Getting Four C's isn't about getting rich. It's about land that's been in my family for generations, about having a place to belong where I have some say."

She realized then how much she was telling him about herself. She hadn't shared many confidences, and she rarely engaged in more than brief, surface conversations. She'd already told Wes more than most people knew and the realization of how much more jolted her. Her alarm must have shown.

"I like it when you talk to me straight out," he said quietly. Hallie could feel his gaze on her tense profile. "I've only been around you a day, but I know already that you interest me. You think there might be something between us?"

It was a shocking question. She turned and took a few restless steps along the creek. "It's best to not…" Sudden, strong emotion silenced her.

"Why?" The calm question hurt. It took several moments to word a truthful answer.

"There are some gambles—" she paused to steady her voice "—that I won't…take." The pain of confessing that was agonizing.

What was happening to her? She'd spent her life keeping silent, hiding what she thought and felt. But there was a torrent of pent-up feeling and unmet need that suddenly seemed impossible to hold back. Something about Wes was weakening her, stealing away small bits of the emotional fortress she couldn't have survived without, and it frightened her.

However much Wes had managed to get her to reveal, he couldn't know the depth of her terror about caring for someone. Love was a mystery. She didn't know how to offer it in a way that ensured acceptance; she had no clue how to attract it. When Wes said he was interested and asked if there could be something between them, it amazed her that he thought she had a choice.

His big hand closed gently on her shoulder and she jumped.

"The way you grew up was wrong," he said gruffly. "Don't let it ruin what you can have from here on."

His kind words were excruciating, and she struggled to harden herself to them. She had to get him off this subject. She had to convince him that she needed neither advice nor sympathy. She turned, mostly to slip from beneath his hand. His touch was so warm and electric that she couldn't breathe.

She made herself give him a neutral look. "The benefit of how I grew up is that I don't have delusions about the way things are, or unreasonable expectations of my place in the world. I don't have foolish ideas about what life's supposed to be."

"Pride won't let you tolerate sympathy, will it? So now you're gonna turn tough on me, let me know you're a cynic too smart for love." He took a moment to let that sink in. "Some women who'd try that might be throwing out a challenge to get me to prove them wrong."

Hallie's face flushed with mortification. "I wouldn't."

His gaze was cool and openly assessing. "I know you wouldn't. You had the grit to come to me and offer a chance to get something we both want, but you'd cut your tongue out before you asked me for anything else. Or dared me to give you the thing that's truly important to you."

"There *is* nothing more important to me than getting Four C's," she insisted shakily.

"You're a liar, Mrs. Lansing."

The ground seemed to shift beneath her feet and she couldn't get a full breath. They'd been together little more than twenty-four hours and Wes was reading her as easily as he would the morning paper. A lifetime of concealing her thoughts and feelings—a lifetime of thinking she was a master at it—was top-pling. She could never trust anyone with the whole truth, but the idea that Wes could somehow discern it anyway panicked her so badly that the world began to spin.

Her soft, "I want the ranch, only the ranch," came out sounding as badly shaken as she felt.

One corner of his strong mouth lifted, but there was no hint of amusement in his dark eyes.

"Then since we'll be sharing my bed, you'll be able to do it and be completely unaffected because you're too tough and cynical and wise to the world to be seduced by trivial things like attraction and proximity. Or hope."

"I can't share your bed." She couldn't get enough air to make her voice sound anything but breathless.

He was relentless. "You have to. So don't look me in the eye and tell me that the only thing you want in life is a piece of land. You'd like to see what could happen between us, but you're so damned terrified of what might *not* happen that you'd rather die of thirst than take a chance on the water. Because the truth is, Halona Lansing, you'd let Four C's go to Candice in a New York minute if someone could guarantee that you could love and be loved. It took stamina and courage to get through your life, and I admire hell out of that, but you're a coward when it comes to going after what you really want."

Her eyes were stinging madly and she was so stirred up and traumatized that her heart was beating out of control. "Why are you doing this?"

The tension went out of him then, and he reached

up to tip his hat back. He searched her stricken expression.

"Musta seen something I thought was worth the trouble to go after." He glanced away from her to the horses. "I'm going back." His attention returned to her. "If you get hungry for something besides Four C's, you might want to have supper with me."

And then he was striding away from her, walking up the bank to check the cinch on his saddle before he mounted up. Hallie followed in a haze of pain and shock. Her hands shook when she saw to her own saddle cinch and climbed into the saddle.

They rode back to the headquarters at a gallop, slowing enough before they reached it to cool the horses.

Wes reverted to silence. Anything he said to her was minimal and brief to the point of terseness. They were strangers again. The time or two that their gazes connected, his was flat and remote. There was no intensity, no perception, no gleam of secret knowledge.

He'd given up on her. Though she'd known it was inevitable, there was a dark wound in her heart that had felt warmed and relieved by the light he'd shone on it. A little like a sick patient who finally finds a competent doctor who can identify the illness and offer a cure.

They'd almost finished eating when the doorbell chimed. Wes had started to rise to answer it when they heard the front door open then close. The quick tap of boot heels echoed on the entry tile. As if he recognized the sound, Wes sat back down. The footsteps approached from the hall and Hallie looked toward the open door.

Elizabeth Lansing Dade stalked over the threshold and came to a sudden halt just inside the door. Her dark gaze shot from Wes at one end of the long table to Hallie who sat at the other.

"Then it's true."

Hallie set her napkin aside. She and Beth had gone through school and graduated together, but Hallie barely knew her. Friendships between their families had been frowned upon.

Beth was delicately beautiful, tall and slender in her crisp white blouse and slacks. She had Wes's dark hair and eyes, but brother and sister had no other features in common.

"Why is it nobody ever heard there was something between you two?" she asked, addressing the question to Wes, but watching Hallie's tense face to gauge her reaction.

Wes tossed his napkin to the table and rose. "I tried to call you this morning from Vegas, but you were out." His dark gaze touched Hallie's briefly. "If we're about to have a family discussion, let's go in and find someplace to sit."

Hallie stood, then started toward the door. Wes joined her and they walked past Beth who turned to follow them to the living room.

Wes left Hallie to seat herself on the sofa and Beth took one of the overstuffed chairs across from her. He went to the liquor cabinet at the side of the room. Hallie waited tensely as Beth asked for a soft drink.

When Wes gave Hallie a raised-brow look to

prompt her choice, she shook her head. He carried the soda to his sister, then came toward the sofa. He sat down so close to Hallie that they touched from shoulder to knee. She tried to look relaxed when he shifted and dropped his arm across her shoulders, but it was impossible.

Beth watched their every move as if she were inspecting a window for flecks of dust. Hallie couldn't help that her fists were clenched together in her lap. Beth took note and didn't keep them waiting.

"So you eloped. Why now and why Hallie *Corbett?*"

Wes's voice was stern. "You tryin' to hint you've never done anything crazy and impetuous and romantic?"

Beth's suspicious look faltered. "That's what you're saying this is?"

His tone was mild, but carried an edge. "Hallie's my wife. Because of family illness, we can't take a honeymoon, but this is our first night home. I didn't expect my kid sister to march in and give me the third degree."

The suspicion about Beth faded to uncertainty. "I'm just so…surprised. And a little hurt that you didn't tell me ahead of time, Wes. I didn't even get to go to the wedding. And she's a—" Beth cut herself off and sent Hallie an uneasy glance before she looked at her brother. "You have to admit, it's strange for you to suddenly marry when no one knew you two had ever exchanged a word. Especially because of the feud."

"You live fifty miles away, sis, and have for the

past four years. You couldn't have counted the words I've exchanged with any of the neighbors. And I'm sorry I didn't let you know ahead of time. It was sudden for us, too.''

Hallie was stricken with guilt. Wes was deceiving his sister to make their marriage look authentic. He wasn't lying precisely, just laying out a logic that supported their agreement to give the look of a real marriage, which at some point won't work out. But it was still deception and it was dishonest. Hallie couldn't bear for him to do this to his sister.

She touched Wes's hand and his fingers caught hers. Her soft, ''Wes?'' made him look at her. He must have read her intent because she saw the glint of caution in his dark eyes before he looked over at his sister.

''So, if I've got it right, good manners would mean giving the bride best wishes and congratulating the groom. Then, maybe a little small talk before we have to leave for the hospital.''

''The hospital?''

''Hallie's grandfather is in Intensive Care.''

Beth showed a flash of remorse. She looked at Hallie. ''I'm sorry, Hallie. I was so…shocked.'' She tried a smile that was sincere but uncertain. ''I hope you and Wes will be happy together. Welcome to our family.''

Hallie's soft, ''Thank you,'' seemed to relieve her, and her smile was a little less uncertain.

''I hope you can forgive me for barging in like this.'' Beth looked at Wes. ''I guess I like to think my big brother needs someone to look out for him from time to time, though he never does." Her gaze came back to Hallie's and went softer. "I shouldn't have worried."

Hallie's quiet, "It's all right," was strained.

Beth's attention shifted to Wes. "I suppose I should slip out of here now and get home."

Wes lifted his arm from Hallie's shoulders and got up. Beth rose. Hallie stood slowly and looked on as Wes wrapped his sister in a big hug and pressed a kiss on the top of her dark head.

"Get goin', brat. And next time, bring that baby. It's been a whole four days. She's gonna forget what her Uncle Wes looks like."

Beth lifted her head and eased back in his arms. "She's only five weeks old, and she's hardly awake long enough when she's been here to know what you look like."

"So you need to bring her around more often, get her so she stays awake when regular people do."

Hallie watched the exchange between brother and sister with secret longing. Wes was a good man and a surprisingly affectionate one. She had to force herself not to stare.

She was so tense that even after Beth was gone, she couldn't relax. "There's no reason for your sister to think this is…real."

Wes turned from the window where he'd been watching Beth get into her car. He gave Hallie a penetrating look.

"It bothers you so much to pretend a real marriage?"

Hallie let out a nervous breath. "Yes. Very much.

And it's worse with your sister. It's not right to deceive her.''

"No, it's not right, but you and I made an agreement."

"We agreed that I would live on Red Thorn and we'd have a public marriage. There's no reason your sister can't know the truth.''

"And what will she have to do if she knows the truth? Do you think she'd like pretending to be a real sister-in-law any better than you like pretending to be a real wife?''

Hallie's heart dropped. Wes changed the subject. "If you're ready, I'll drive you to the hospital.''

CHAPTER FIVE

WHEN they got to the ICU, they learned that Hank had recovered from his light coma more than two hours before and was lucid enough to refuse visitors. Candice hadn't come to the hospital at all.

On their ride back to Red Thorn, Hallie was torn between worry and relief. Worry that their marriage might have to go on indefinitely; relief that Hank was doing better. It didn't matter that he'd treated her poorly all these years, she'd never wanted him to die. And selfishly, she couldn't quit hoping for something from him, some word or sign that he'd felt something for her in spite of all he'd done to hurt her.

She was exhausted by the stress of the past two days, but the thought of going back to Red Thorn twisted her in knots. When Wes pulled his car to a halt at the end of the ranch mansion's front walk, he switched off the engine and glanced her way.

"You aren't going to an execution, Hallie. I don't expect sex." The soft amusement in his low voice sent a flash of heat to her face.

"You don't respect me or you wouldn't demand this."

His gaze went solemn. "I respect *my wife* enough to insist that she sleeps where a wife is supposed to sleep."

Feeling trapped, Hallie looked away from him. He

reached across the seat to touch her arm and she winced before she caught herself.

"However things turn out with Hank, you're my wife. I plan to treat you like my wife."

Hallie looked over at him. "In *public*. Your bedroom is private."

"It is. But Candice will move heaven and earth to find out who sleeps where on Red Thorn. We have two other people who live under the same roof."

"Don't you expect loyalty and confidentiality from the people who work for you?"

"I do, but I can't coach them on how to behave or how to answer someone who tries to trick information out of them. It's easier for them if they think things are normal between us." He gave her a close look. "And how could I tell the hired help something I don't plan to tell my own sister?"

"H-how will we get an annulment?" she persisted shakily. "If people know we sleep together, they'll assume…" She couldn't finish.

"Annulment worked only as long as the marriage was secret and we never lived together. The minute Edna Murray caught us in Vegas wearing wedding clothes on our way to a room, we lost the chance to make a credible claim to a sexless marriage."

The grimness in his gaze made her glance away from him, panicked. Divorce. Neither of them spoke the word aloud, but it thundered in the warming air of the parked car.

"It's not the end of the world, Hallie."

Heartsick and agitated, Hallie levered open her door and got out.

Wes knew he was witnessing terror. Though outwardly, Hallie's face was as smooth as polished marble, he felt her fear like a low-level vibration.

They'd taken turns showering and both were now dressed for bed. He normally slept nude, but that was out of the question tonight, so he wore a pair of pajama bottoms that had languished in a drawer for years. Hallie was wearing a blue, lightweight flannel nightgown that covered her from throat to toe, and the out-of-season sleepwear gave her a look of imperiled virginity. He'd pretended not to notice, but he'd turned down the air-conditioning to accommodate her. It was likely the only thing he could do to make her feel more comfortable.

Wes casually flipped down the bedspread and top sheet, ignoring the flicker of dread in Hallie's eyes as her face paled. He got into bed and pulled the covers over himself, alert for the moment she worked up her courage and slid into bed beside him.

That moment stretched so long and was fraught with so much tension that he almost relented, but instinct warned him to be firm. She was like a young horse who'd been brutalized and left to run wild; she needed to learn that not everyone was a threat, that there were people she could trust. And just like that wounded young horse, she guarded herself too closely to ever come in from the range unless someone made the effort to bring her in.

When she finally crawled into bed beside him, she took care to do so in a way that kept the hem of her long nightgown secure at her ankles. She laid back self-consciously on the pillow and covered up, but her body was so rigid she was in danger of shattering. Wes switched off the lamp. He allowed her to keep a distance, but her increased tension in the darkness made him realize she might bolt from the bed if he so much as blinked.

"Only a cold-blooded criminal would force sex on a woman who doesn't want it, Halona," he said quietly. "We don't know yet if there are sexual feelings between us that are important enough to act on."

He heard her quick, shallow breathing hitch faintly. Her soft voice carried a hint of indignation. "I'm inexperienced, but I'm not stupid. A man and a woman who sleep together—"

"Tell you what, darlin'," he cut in coolly, "let me know the minute you think you can't keep your hands off me. I'll let you know then if I'm in the mood to do anything about it."

He turned away from her and expelled a weary sigh as he adjusted his pillow and settled down to sleep. He felt the shock wave of her surprise. A small movement told him she'd turned her head on her pillow to gape at him. Her stillness signaled she was thinking over what he'd said, that she didn't know how to take him.

Good. He'd meant to give her something to think about. He'd pushed her hard, but now he was backing off because she seemed to respond to that. Just like he'd do with that young horse he kept comparing her to, pushing her a little then easing up gave her a chance to check herself and decide if she'd been hurt. Or if she'd ever been in peril in the first place. And just like that young horse, somewhere along the line it would dawn on her that she felt a little safer with him, a little more comfortable.

Because he'd like to get to know the woman he'd married. The vows he'd spoken in that chapel the night before seemed too weighty to easily dismiss. And the longer he was around Halona Corbett Lansing, the more he understood how remarkable it was that she'd spoken those vows with him—with anyone—at all.

Hallie couldn't relax. It'd been years since she'd slept in a house with other people. To find herself lying in a bed next to Wes traumatized her.

She knew he wouldn't force himself on her; she'd always known that somehow. But she remembered what he'd told her on the creek bank about what she really wanted.

Did he know how she'd felt when he'd kissed her? Had he guessed that she craved another kiss almost as much as she was terrified to have one? Did he know how easy it might be to seduce her?

Inexperience and confusion made everything so much worse. She didn't know how to act, and she worried that everything she might do would be wrong. From the moment she'd got her copy of the Will and set out to inherit Four C's, she'd made one mistake after another, until the catastrophes piled up and she couldn't figure out how to stop them.

And now she had to cope with this, lying next to Wes, feeling the heat of his big body scorch her from shoulder to foot, though inches of empty mattress separated them. She could hear the deep, steady sound of his breathing—so much heavier than her own quiet breath—and she was sharply aware of his powerful presence.

His tough, rugged masculinity overwhelmed her and she was helpless to dispel the nervous flush that had settled over her skin and seemed to burn everywhere. Her insides tingled peculiarly and the memory of his mouth on hers—the memory of the taste of him—was suddenly so fresh and distinct that she jerked her fingers to her lips to rub the sensation away.

What if she fell asleep and rolled against him?

It was loneliness that made her fear that. Loneliness and the unsatisfied craving to love and be loved that was so increasingly hard to suppress. What if she fell asleep and some desperate impulse came fully to the surface? She realized exhaustion had magnified her worries, but being so far out of her element made it impossible to stop her anxious thoughts.

We don't know yet if there are sexual feelings between us that are important enough to act on, he'd told her before he'd added the almost bored, *Let me know the minute you think you can't keep your hands off me. I'll let you know then if I'm in the mood to do anything about it.*

Truth to tell, he hadn't acted as if he were much attracted to her at all, before or after his kisses. Which was why she was terrified she'd turn toward him in her sleep and do something he wouldn't welcome, some nameless something she couldn't imagine with her limited knowledge of sexuality.

And so she laid stiffly beside Wes, haunted. She

couldn't help that her chest hurt and a flood of pain came up to strangle her and make her eyes sting. She was every bit the misfit her grandfather had said.

The tenderness Wes felt for his wife made him take special care not to startle her that next morning. Exhaustion had overtaken her by four a.m., and she'd finally fallen so deeply asleep that she hadn't been disturbed when he'd turned toward her and pulled her against him.

She'd so worn herself out by dozing lightly, then jerking awake over any small hint of sound or faint movement he'd made, that she hadn't known it when he'd pillowed her cheek on one arm, smoothed her glorious hair between them, then slid his other arm around her waist.

They'd both slept deeply after that, but now it was almost nine a.m. The sunlight streaming in the bedroom's east windows had woke him a few minutes ago, but Hallie had only just stirred.

He'd switched off the alarm clock on the bed table during the night when he'd realized that neither of them were getting any rest. If he hadn't, the most they'd have gotten was an hour's sleep. Hallie was too on edge about everything not to be further worn down by it.

Besides, sleeping late had spoiled her plan to work on Four C's. She was strong-willed enough to defy his wishes about that, so her difficulty falling asleep had made it easier to get his way. He knew there was another confrontation ahead on the subject, but she'd lost this round.

* * *

Hallie was surrounded by hard warmth, but she didn't feel trapped. She felt safe, secure, content. Rare, precious feelings, and she clung to them, loath to wake up.

Her palm rubbed lazily over a muscle-corded forearm with warm, hair-studded skin. A blind encounter with the heel of a large hand made her push her fingers into the callused palm. Guided by a pleasant impulse, her fingertips skidded lightly across that hard palm and laced easily with steely fingers so large and strong that when they flexed gently to curl over the back of her hand, she felt the quiet thrill of acceptance.

The raspy whisper at her ear brought her fully awake. "Good morning, Halona."

Hallie went rigid. Wes gripped her hand and his arm tightened at her waist to keep her firmly against him. She felt his hard body along every inch of her back and thighs, and was suddenly aware of every masculine detail.

"I'm afraid to let you go," he went on softly, his warm breath gusting across the shell of her ear to send a shower of sensation through her. "I don't want you to jump out of this bed and go back to being stiff and afraid to touch me."

Something almost wistful in his soft tone soothed her nerves, but she'd barely registered it before the arm at her waist relaxed and the fingers that were gently laced with hers went slack. Because she wasn't sure what he expected her to do, she hesitated, then pulled her hand from his and pushed back the covers to slip from beneath his arm. She sat up and slid to the edge of the bed but stopped there and glanced back at him uncertainly.

The covers came only to his waist leaving his wide, muscular chest bare. He rose up on an elbow and one corner of his mouth quirked.

"You're looking at me different. Is that a good sign?" He smiled faintly, his dark eyes warm. The combination of warmth and bare, hair-sprinkled male chest against a background of rumpled bedding seemed profoundly sexy to her inexperienced gaze.

"I—I hope." The daring confession sent a tide of heat to her face, but she saw the glint of approval in his dark gaze. He reached up and touched her cheek. The gesture seemed so natural and easy between them that the only thing she felt was the shivering sweetness of his warm fingers.

"Spend the day with me, Hallie. See what it's like on this side of the fence."

It was surprising how hard it was to shift her gaze from his to the sunlit east windows to check the time.

"It's after nine," he said as the late hour registered. "Quickest you could get there now would be ten or ten-thirty, but everyone would expect you to spend time with your new husband."

Hallie couldn't help the embarrassment she felt. She thought about the rugged men she worked alongside day in and day out. Men who joked with each other about sex and Saturday nights in town when they thought she was out of earshot.

She hadn't thought until just that moment how hard it would be to face them when they thought she was a true bride who'd had a wedding night. They'd never say anything to her directly, but that thought put her only marginally at ease.

If she showed up so soon after getting married, would they speculate on that behind her back? If they saw her as the man-shy misfit Hank did, it was entirely possible that her quick return to work might make her the target of other kinds of secret jokes and innuendo. And though they'd never intend for her to overhear, it was inevitable she'd catch some of it.

Her gaze came back to his and she felt a niggle of helplessness that shamed her. Wes had asked her to spend the day with him, but what would they do? What if she bored him? And why was it suddenly so monumentally important that he enjoy being with her? She didn't have a clue how to make herself either enjoyable or likable.

He tipped his head back slightly to give her a penetrating look. ''Your eyes are such a changeable blue. Sometimes they go light—not often. Sometimes they get dark, shadowy. Like now.'' He paused, then said quietly, ''It's a new day, Halona. Some things are possible, some things aren't. I'm only asking you to spend the day with me.''

Emotions she refused to identify came rushing up. Her soft, ''All right,'' was choked.

She'd never brushed her hair in front of a man before. She'd never watched a man lather his face with a shaving brush, then shave. Sharing Wes's big bathroom while they performed those morning rituals had given her such unexpected pleasure that her worries about spending the day with him eased.

He'd persuaded her to leave her hair unbraided. She'd waited until he'd finished shaving and left the bathroom before she'd lightly applied a few of the cosmetics she'd bought in Las Vegas. When she surveyed her efforts in the mirror, she was pleased for those first moments before self-consciousness overcame her. There was no denying that the more she became aware of Wes as a man, the more feminine she wanted to be.

It struck her that for the first in her life, she might be free to be something more than the neglected tomboy kept firmly in the shadow of a beautiful cousin who was the epitome of femininity, free to be something more than the child who didn't dare reveal herself.

As Hallie stared into that wide pristine mirror, she could see for herself that a change had begun, a change that had the potential to go far deeper than cosmetics.

The certainty that her marriage to Wes—that Wes himself—had somehow been the catalyst for this change was undeniable. It had started the moment she'd walked into his office with that Will in her hands and his dark gaze had impacted hers.

And now that she was living with him away from the oppression of her family, she felt an amazing freedom to explore who she might be, to discover who she was. It was as if she'd walked out into sunshine from a small dark room that had been her prison all her life.

But she was still wary of the sunlight. It felt too new and she was too unsure of herself to be completely comfortable. As she put the cosmetics back into the drawer and gave herself a last look, she decided she was pleased with this small start.

What had Wes said? *It's a new day, Halona. Some things are possible, some things aren't.*

With her heart made lighter by the thought of possibilities, Hallie turned from the mirror to hurry down to breakfast.

As traumatic as falling asleep with Wes had been, waking up in his arms had deeply affected her. She felt a closeness to him now, a level of trust she wouldn't have thought possible. As they sat at the table on the back veranda that looked over the patio and pool, Hallie felt surprisingly at ease with him as they shared a late breakfast.

His rugged appeal seemed more intense somehow. She was more aware of his big body, the power of it, his male grace. Her skin still tingled with the memory of sliding her fingers across his hard palm to lace with his fingers. Every time she looked at him, she felt a stroke of heat as she recalled the warm hard feel of his body against hers.

"I had your car put in the garage," he told her as he cut through his breakfast steak. "Drive the Cadillac if you need a car. The keys are in the ignition. Unless you'd rather use the Suburban."

The words startled her from her thoughts and made her realize she'd been staring at him. He apparently hadn't noticed, because it was only now, when she didn't automatically respond about the car, that he glanced over at her, prompting her to speak.

"I'd...rather not." Though her car wasn't a Cadillac or a sport utility vehicle, it was respectable. Was he concerned about the appearance if his wife drove something less elegant?

Wes gave her a searching look. "Mind telling me why you'd rather not?"

"I pay my own way," she said simply, then had a bite of fluffy egg.

"I didn't run to town and buy that Cadillac or Suburban specifically for you, but you live in my house, sleep in my bed, and you're sharing my life," he said reasonably. "Makes sense to me that driving my cars is part of that."

Sharing my life. Words that suddenly rose up like a dazzling mirage on a sunbaked highway and sent a spear of pain through her heart. They were living together, not sharing their lives. Not really.

But something about those words was suddenly so sacred to her that she couldn't bring herself to voice a correction.

"I don't own much more than the nearest cowhand," she said quietly. "I don't want anyone to say that I married you for your money or that I couldn't wait to grab all the advantages."

"That why you insisted on buying your own things in Vegas?"

Hallie went stiff. "A bride is supposed to buy her own dress."

"A *wife* is entitled to have access to the things her husband owns."

He sounded so decisive, as if he was making a point about normal marital expectations. She was afraid he might be hinting at expectations she couldn't allow and she rushed to discourage that.

"A real wife would. But we signed a prenuptial agreement."

"You're a real wife, Halona. So real it'll take a real divorce to change that. The prenup defines who has claim to what, if it comes to that."

If it comes to that. Those were the words that rocked her. She was suddenly so flustered that the fork trembled wildly in her fingers. She set it down to keep from dropping it.

"W-why do you say things like that?" The words were out before she realized.

He leaned back and watched her flushed face as if he'd been waiting for this. His voice went low and there was a disturbing quietness in it that signaled he was about to probe deep.

"Things like what? Things like *if* it comes to divorce?"

Hallie didn't answer because they both knew what she meant. If she kept silent, maybe he'd stop there. But then she saw the sudden depth in his dark eyes and knew it was a futile hope.

"Maybe I think things have changed since that chapel in Vegas," he said, his bluntness underscoring a level of sincerity that blindsided her. "We rushed into this thinking we knew how it'd work out, and got a big surprise. So I'm going to think long and hard before I rush into divorce."

She was nearly breathless. "There's nothing to think about."

"I think there is." His absolute certainty was something she was compelled to fight.

"You don't mean that the way it sounds."

"What does it sound like?"

The words burst up from sudden yearning. "Like...you think you could lo—" She cut herself off, mortified. "That this could be a permanent marriage."

"I told you from the first that you needed to learn that I mean what I say."

Hallie plucked her napkin off her lap and put it on the table. She was so agitated that she stood up, not caring that her breakfast was only half finished. Wes tossed his napkin to the table and stood, his lean height looming across from her in some silent signal that suggested he'd come after her if she bolted. His intensity seemed to reach across the table and envelop her in a tight grip.

"Why are you so threatened, Halona?"

Hallie was breathing hard, as if she'd just sprinted a quarter mile, so stirred up she could barely stand still. He was torturing her, running sharp rowels across her heart, cutting into her deepest needs.

Only it wasn't blood that welled into the cuts, but the acid of knowing that he might play at marriage a while, he might even seriously consider her suitability as a wife. But in the end, he'd reject her. If he got too close, he'd discover that mysterious failing that made her unlovable, and he'd cast her away from him as easily as he would a shirt that didn't fit right.

"Halona?" His voice was quiet, almost somber.

"I've lived my whole life one way," she told him,

barely able to keep the angry tremor out of her voice. "You aren't going to change that. I'm not willing to play at some trial marriage when you and I both know this will end."

"How do we know?"

The patient question lanced deep into places that might never heal, places so raw that she couldn't help the instant, "I'm not what you want."

A faint curve touched his strong mouth. "I don't even know for sure yet what I want. How can you know? You got a crystal ball someplace?"

What was left of those warm sweet feelings she'd had that morning burned away like light dew beneath a merciless sun. The closeness she'd felt toward him turned out to be the Trojan horse of a conqueror bent on total invasion. Strangling emotion made it impossible to speak.

Wes's faint smile faded as he pushed on with a relentlessness that made her head go light. "When you showed up here two days ago offering me a chance to get the homestead back, I decided to take the bargain because of *you,* not the land." His stern gaze gentled on her pale face. "If you hadn't intrigued hell out of me and given me one of the strongest flashes of lust I've ever felt, I would have turned you down cold and forgotten what you looked like five minutes after you'd gone home."

"S-stop." The word was as breathless as she felt. Her insides were twisting with fear and pain and longing, and she wasn't certain she could hold herself together.

"I don't feel a speck of ill will toward you, Halona. I'm asking you for time and maybe a chance."

It was the tenderness in his voice and the gentle sincerity in his dark eyes that nearly finished her off. She glanced away from him, fighting madly to still the confusing chaos of hunger and emotion he'd dredged up.

"Please...sit down with me. Finish your breakfast." His low voice was a rasp. "I didn't mean to upset you. I'm sorry."

I'm sorry. Words she'd rarely heard, words that magically dulled every sharp edge of pain he'd inflicted. But he hadn't truly inflicted pain on her, he'd merely uncovered it and exposed it to them both. She must seem pitiful to him.

It was pride that saved her a precious sliver of ego. If she escaped him now, he'd know the extent of what he'd done. If she stayed, tried to finish eating and forced herself back to something resembling normal, she might be able to brazen it out, make him think she'd merely been angry, rather than very nearly devastated by the impossible lure of a chance at love.

Her shaking knees made it easier to sit. She couldn't look at him. She reached for her napkin and spread it across her lap. When he spoke, her gaze jerked up to his, then away.

"I'll be looking over the two-year-olds we brought in a couple days ago. They need to be started in the next few days."

Work talk. Safe talk. Hallie tried to eat, but the effort was mechanical at first. The steady, casual sound of Wes's voice as he laid out his plans for the young horses soothed her roiling emotions. She couldn't allow herself to think about why the gruff timbre of his low voice affected her like that.

By the time she was able to fully relax, they were on their way to the pasture to the west of the corrals. They'd got only a few feet away from the back patio when Marie came rushing out to call Hallie to the phone.

CHAPTER SIX

"TELL him I'm on my way."

Hallie hung up the phone in the den. The foreboding that had made her rush into the house to take the call from the hospital had eased to simple dread. According to the nurse Hank had selected to make the call, he was doing remarkably better. So much better that he'd ordered Hallie to the hospital—to the private room they'd just moved him into—right away.

This morning had been difficult enough, but now she had to face her grandfather well before regular visiting hours. Hank would expect her to give an account of her actions. He'd take great satisfaction in shredding her to ribbons before he announced that she was out of the will.

Nevertheless, Hank's improvement was a relief. Whether he'd ever know it or not, changing his Will to leave her out would take a load of guilt off her heart. She'd no longer have a financial stake in when he passed away. And now that her marriage to Wes had become so complicated, being written out of the will right away would free them both just that much sooner.

"How's he doing?"

Wes's voice from the open doorway let her know he'd followed her in. She kept her back to him and forced a neutral tone.

"Doing well enough to be out of Intensive Care. He wants me at the hospital right away."

"I'll drive you."

Hallie shook her head. "No, thank you."

"You shouldn't go alone."

Hallie took a shallow breath and turned toward him. "I've been going alone to the hospital every day for the past month, sometimes twice a day," she pointed out calmly.

"You just married me. Hank knows it by now."

"Which was why he had someone call me. At least I know he'll let me in the room."

"I don't want you to go alone," he said, and she couldn't miss the steely edge in his voice. "If he's rough on you, I don't want you driving."

Hallie's gaze wavered from his. Hank would be in a lather over their marriage and she'd be facing a new ordeal when she went to visit him. But she couldn't mistake Wes's concern. He'd already made it clear that what she did and what might be done to her reflected on him now. Because she was his wife and she bore the Lansing name, it was probably more some macho ownership thing rather than anything truly personal.

She couldn't allow herself to think it was something more. Survival dictated that she distance herself from Wes, to reassert the emotional independence she couldn't function without. She forced herself to meet his gaze and appear unconcerned.

"What could he possibly say to me that would be more traumatic than anything else he's ever said? The only new thing he can say this time is, 'You're out of the Will, you'll never get Four C's.'"

Wes regarded her with an intensity that made her anxiety rise. "Won't that be hard to take? He'll probably have some choice things to say about marrying a Lansing."

His persistence frustrated her. She knew better than anyone what she was in for. The last thing she wanted to cope with was presenting an unruffled facade to a man who'd demonstrated an almost psychic ability to read her.

Hallie mustered a smile that felt stiff. "I don't need a protector."

He gave her a narrow look. "What you don't want is a witness."

This time, his accuracy sent a hot streak of resentment through her. "That's right, Lansing. So why don't you get the message and back off?"

It ranked as the most petulant thing she'd ever said in her life. When she saw the flicker of surprise in his eyes, she realized he hadn't expected it.

But then, why would he have expected it? So far, he'd been able to push and probe at her, almost at will. He'd gotten his way on nearly everything, even on things she was uncomfortable with. Like pressuring her to confide in him. Like insisting she share his bed.

In spite of what he'd said about losing their independence in that Vegas chapel, she couldn't afford to give hers up. Now was the time to demonstrate that.

"I'm going to the hospital. Alone."

Wes's gaze flared darkly, then went cool. "All right, Halona. You're on your own."

Hallie hadn't been able to calm herself on the ride to the hospital. Of all the times she'd had to face Hank Corbett's displeasure, only a very few of them had made her palms sweat. She had to chafe them briskly on her jeans to keep them dry. The breakfast she'd forced down sat like a rock in her stomach, and the antacids she'd chewed had no discernible effect on the fire that threatened to burn a hole through her insides.

She was about to lose her only chance to get Four C's. Another tantalizing scrap would be yanked from reach, and she had to give Hank the impression that it didn't matter to her, that she was impervious to pain.

Hallie stopped a few feet from the door of Hank's private room and struggled to school her features into a mask of calm. Wes had shaken her confidence in being able to hide her feelings. It helped a little to remember that Wes was far more perceptive than either Hank or Candice. Possibly because his perceptiveness was based more on an inclination to understand rather than a predatory search for weakness.

The reminder increased her regret about what she'd said to him. Perhaps he'd been genuinely concerned for her after all. In spite of the way he pressed her to reveal herself, he'd been surprisingly gentle with her. She shouldn't have lost her temper, she shouldn't have rebuffed him that harshly. She'd known from the first that he was domineering, but his brand of dominance wasn't necessarily objectionable.

Forcing thoughts of Wes away, she took more moments to relax. Deep breaths helped only marginally. In the end, she made herself walk through the door into Hank's room with a confident stride that was little more than playacting.

Hank Corbett was propped up on a hospital bed that had been motored into a sitting position. Candice fussed with his pillows. The private nurse who sat nearby glanced Hallie's way, then quietly rose and slipped out of the room. Candice looked over and gave Hallie a feline smile.

"Look who's here, Granddaddy."

Hank turned his head toward Hallie. His stern gaze met hers and glinted. "Get on over here," he said harshly, "and gimme a look at *Mrs. Wes Lansing.*"

Hallie fought to keep her breathing steady as she walked to his bed and stopped at the side opposite Candice. "Hello, Hank. You're looking better."

And he did. His gray eyes were clear and sharp. His angular face had lost its unhealthy pallor, and there was a spark of energy about him that suggested a recovery from illness. The change shocked her. Had the doctors been wrong about his grim prognosis?

"Candy's been after Lansing since she figured out boys and girls were made different, but *you* got 'im." The old man chuckled at that and the harshness in him vanished.

Hallie felt her cousin's sudden outrage, but didn't

let her gaze veer from the odd cheer in Hank's as he went on.

"Never thought I'd see the day the little tomboy could do something smart and sly that Candy couldn't," he crowed. "I underestimated you, girl."

Hallie jumped when Hank caught her hand in a warm grip. "You been hidin' your light under a bushel."

It was all she could do to allow his touch. She felt dazed, as if she'd walked into an alternative universe. Her gaze slid to Candice to see that her cousin was even more shocked than she was.

"B-but Granddaddy," Candice sputtered, "she as much as knifed you in the back."

"Sure she did," he agreed, but the wide grin on his face was one of delight. "She thought I was cuttin' her out of something she wanted and she didn't take it lyin' down."

Hallie stared at her grandfather, stunned. He beamed with the approval she'd hungered for her whole life, but his reason for finally giving it dawned on her degree by appalling degree.

"You've given me a new lease on life, Halona," he went on. "It took guts and guile to snare Lansing and put a ring through his nose. Now we've got some interesting potentials."

Horrified, Hallie tried to withdraw her hand, but Hank's fingers tightened like a vise. The moment he felt her rings, he pulled her closer to look at them.

"And would you look at that rock," he chortled before his wide grin vanished and he shot Candice a cagey look. "How many times have I told you that a clever woman can parlay her virginity into a fortune?''

The utter distaste of that sent a wave of horror over Hallie and a stinging heat to her face. The unabashed calculation that motivated every word out of her grandfather's mouth gave a stark impression of evil that she'd never seen this strongly or this close up. Because she'd been excluded from the almost obsessive relationship between Hank and Candice, she'd rarely experienced anything more diabolical than the hurtful things they'd directed at her.

The sense that Hank had finally accepted her wholeheartedly into the Corbett family circle—and the level of cunning that acceptance must have required—sent such a sickness through her that it was all she could do to breathe.

"Candice is right," she got out, desperate to correct Hank's bizarre conclusions about her marriage to Wes. "I was disloyal to you. I married Wes thinking you'd die before you could change your Will. Having it come out was accidental or you'd never have known.''

Hank's attention snapped back to her and he went still. His sharp gaze searched hers. "And that's proof you're as much a Corbett as any of us," he said, and nodded with satisfaction. "A Corbett fights, clean or dirty, any and all who try to take what's theirs. I don't hold that against you, so I'm giving you Four C's.'' A smile of anticipation lit his gaunt features. "In the meantime, we'll see what else you can do now that you've got your rope on Lansing." His grip tightened affectionately. "I can't think of a stronger incentive to fight the Grim Reaper."

Hallie felt the world take another sharp spin as her brain whirled with the shock of it all. Her knees barely held her up. She didn't realize Hank had pulled her down to him until he gave the gruff order, "Give your granddaddy a kiss for luck."

As if she'd suddenly become a robot, she found herself pressing a stiff kiss to his lean cheek before she straightened, shocked that she'd done it. Hank had never demanded or given her a single sign of affection. That she'd given him one now under these circumstances and at his order filled her with self-loathing. She tried to pull her cold fingers from his, but he gave them a firm squeeze before he released them.

"You run along home to Lansing. Keep him happy and distracted. I'll be thinkin' on what your next move oughtta be."

Hallie stared at her grandfather's face, searching in vain for a sign that this was all some twisted joke. Her gaze shifted sluggishly to Candice, but the pink-tinged rage on her cousin's face told her that if this was a joke, Candice wasn't part of it.

When she suddenly found herself outside Hank's hospital room, Hallie realized she felt otherworldly and disoriented. She walked down the long corridor, so staggered by the scope of what had just happened that she doubted her sanity. She'd made it out of the hospital into the sobering heat of midday when a manicured hand clamped painfully on her arm and jerked her to a halt.

Candice stepped in front of her, her beautiful features livid as she hissed, "You little Judas. Hank's had too much medication to know what's really going on, but I'll make him see it. You've no more got Wes Lansing twisted around your little finger than I do."

"I never claimed to."

Candice leaned closer, her voice on the verge of going shrill. "And *you* have no claim to *anything* Corbett. My daddy's the one the Corbett line went through—*I'm* the Corbett heir. You'd never have had the Corbett name if your mama's one-night stand had stayed in bed with her long enough to ask who she was."

The insult to her mother sent an explosion of anger through Hallie that cleared the shock from her brain. She threw off Candice's painful grip. She kept her voice carefully even. "So, are we trading insults to our mothers? If we are, then I wonder if both of us would show Corbett DNA if Hank decided to order a blood test?"

The horror on Candice's face gave her less satisfaction than she'd thought. Insults were Candice's forte, not hers. She ignored the ones Candice dealt to her on a regular basis, but she wouldn't tolerate insults to her late mother. If that brought her down to Candice's level, so be it. Dimly, Hallie realized her sudden militancy was a result of deep emotional upset. On the other hand, perhaps it was time to stand up to Candice in a way she understood.

Candice recovered and gave her a calculating look. "All right, cousin," she began, nodding as if satisfied with some decision she'd just made. "Like

Granddaddy said, 'A Corbett fights, clean or dirty, any and all who try to take what's theirs.' You're trying to take what's mine. If you plan to keep the things that are yours, you'd better get them moved off Four C's by two o'clock today. That includes those nags of yours that might be accidentally loaded on a truck for the slaughterhouse by two-thirty.''

''Fine,'' Hallie said coolly, frustrated because it was after twelve-thirty and she had no doubt that Candice would make good the threat to her horses. ''Since you haven't given me the luxury of time, I assume you'll be generous enough to allow me to use a Four C's truck and stock trailer.''

Candice smiled brittlely. ''Go ahead. But bring them back by three or I'll call the sheriff and file a theft complaint.''

Hallie stepped past her and stalked to her car, so stirred up that her head began to pound.

Hallie drove the truck and long stock trailer past the front entrance at Four C's five minutes before two o'clock. She'd got one of the wranglers from the stable to drive her car to Red Thorn, and she was no more than five minutes behind him.

A mile down the highway, she heard a siren and went tense. A quick check of the pickup's side mirror confirmed that there were no vehicles except the county squad car for miles ahead or behind her.

When the cruiser caught up and moved into the lane beside the pickup, she slowed the truck and carefully eased it to the highway shoulder to stop. She kept track of the stock trailer behind that carried the last of her things from the house, plus the three horses she owned and their tack.

She reached for her handbag as fresh anger began to build. If she'd been thinking straight at the hospital, she would have been more wary of Candice's easy permission to use a Four C's truck and trailer. Instead, she'd let herself be suckered into a neat little demonstration of Candice's ability to harass.

She summoned a smile for the deputy who came to her door. "Good afternoon, Deputy. Is something wrong? I didn't think I was speeding."

Belatedly she noted that he rested his hand on his holster in a manner that suggested he might regard her as a threat.

"Please step out of the truck, Miz Corbett."

His no-nonsense demeanor suggested strong disapproval, and Hallie opened the truck door to comply.

Once she'd stepped out, the officer spoke. "I'll have to take you in for this. You've got the right to remain silent...."

The fact that his wife hadn't been the one to inform him of her arrest made Wes even more furious. By the time he stalked into the sheriff's office with the ownership papers for her horses and arranged for Hallie's release, his temper simmered at a low boil. He'd already paid a visit to the county attorney and applied enough pressure to ensure that the theft charges against Hallie would be dropped and the arrest expunged.

But tomorrow morning the town newspaper and

most of the daily papers over central and west Texas would be carrying the story of Halona Corbett Lansing's arrest for horse and car theft. Though they'd also be obliged to report that the false charges would be dropped, the fact that the story would end up in print gave fresh notoriety to the Corbett-Lansing feud.

He didn't give a rip about the Corbett part of that, but he hated that the Lansing name was linked to something that might amount to a catfight between cousins. Perhaps Hallie was right. Maybe she wasn't what he wanted. Wes realized that a large part of the anger he felt now was because he'd thought she might be.

Hallie sat rigidly in the small interrogation room. It was an improvement over the jail cell, but she must have been considered a dangerous criminal, because the deputy had put her in handcuffs for the move, but hadn't taken them off.

Of all the shaming events she'd suffered at Candice's hand, this one was by far the most public and the most demeaning. She absently rubbed her fingers on her jeans, as if the repeated friction of skin against denim could wear away the traces of black that lingered from being fingerprinted.

The truck and trailer had been impounded and her horses stabled. No one had been able to tell her whether she'd be formally arraigned for theft, and the lawyer she'd called hadn't put in an appearance.

The sheriff himself had questioned her once she'd waived her right to an attorney, but she had no idea if he'd believed her. He'd asked about ownership papers for the three horses, but those were in the box of legal papers she and Wes had taken to Red Thorn. Her hope that she could handle the frivolous arrest on her own without involving Wes had ended the moment the Sheriff told her he'd call Wes to bring the papers in.

Why don't you get the message and back off? The cross words she'd said to Wes started another monotonous refrain in her mind. His terse, *You're on your own,* rang in her head like the chorus.

If she'd ignored Hank's Will, accepted the loss of Four C's and made plans to leave for a fresh start someplace else, she'd never have gone to Wes. If she'd never gone to Wes, she'd never have set in motion the chain of calamities that had culminated in her arrest.

And the calamities wouldn't stop there. She still had to face Wes, still had to face the consequences of her rash bid to be independent of him when, as his wife, she'd owed him the courtesy of involvement in any action that had the potential to bring scandal to his name.

She should have risked taking time to go to Red Thorn for a truck and trailer. If she'd allowed Wes to go to the hospital with her in the first place, she doubted she and Candice would have clashed. If she'd dreamed Candice would go this far...

The scuff of boot heels outside the small room sent a fresh wave of anxiety through her. She drew her wrists tighter together in her lap in a vain attempt to conceal the handcuffs and took a quick breath. The door swung inward and Wes preceded the sheriff into the room.

Hallie had endured hard looks before, but the brutal look on Wes's rugged face made her shiver almost convulsively. Cold fire blazed so deep in his dark eyes that he must have been burning up with fury; his mouth was set in such a tight, straight line that it might have been a slash gouged into granite. The terrible control in the way he moved suggested barely restrained violence. His low voice was quiet, but the sound of it was somehow a warning instead of the laconic greeting it pretended to be.

"Halona."

What did she really know about Wes Lansing? After the sanity-shattering visit to her grandfather that day, she realized she trusted everyone less. Though she'd known her grandfather was a cruel man, she hadn't fully realized until today how far his potential for evil went or how extensively it had pervaded his thinking.

Could she have missed a potential for violence in Wes Lansing? Was the way he looked now the beginning of another traumatic revelation? The nausea she'd battled successfully for hours surged.

The sheriff walked toward her with the cuff keys. "Miz Lansing? I'm releasing you pending the complete drop of the charges."

Hallie rose to her feet and stiffly held out her wrists for the sheriff to unlock the cuffs. She couldn't look at Wes as the sheriff went on.

"I advise you to stay on Red Thorn until this all gets cleared up. And I'd steer clear of Miz Corbett. If you've got anything else you need to get from Four

C's, you call me and I'll personally arrange a time to go with you.'' He paused and Hallie nodded. "I hope you understand that the deputy was doin' the job the way he thought he should.''

Hallie nodded again. "I doubt I'll be filing a complaint against this office, Sheriff.'' As if Wes's silent anger was a magnet, her gaze skipped to his then away. In that scant second, the tough, harsh look on his face and the hard lights in his eyes had imprinted themselves on her brain like a photograph.

She started toward the door and felt the pressure of Wes's presence behind her as she exited the room. One of the deputies in the outer office got her attention and motioned her toward the counter where her handbag had been stored.

Her soft, "What about my horses and belongings?'' was answered by the officer as he handed over her purse. "Mr. Lansing's taken care of that.''

Hallie gripped her handbag, then slung the strap to her shoulder. As she crossed through the squad room toward the front door of the building, Wes maintained his silent escort beside her. Once she stepped out into the lingering heat of early evening, he took her arm and altered her direction toward his parked car. Though his touch was firm, it was gentle, and her nerve endings sizzled with electricity.

Neither of them spoke. Wes opened her door for her, then closed it with a snap when she got in. She made a quick study of his iron profile as he crossed in front of the car to go to the driver's side. When he got in, he pushed the key into the ignition, gave it a twist, then buckled his seat belt and checked for traffic before he backed out of the parking slot.

Each movement he made was calm, almost careful, but the anger radiating from him buffeted her. Nausea climbed higher in her chest as they reached the highway and Wes smoothly accelerated.

They were almost to Red Thorn before he broke the silence. "Dora's keeping supper for us."

Hallie sent a cautious glance his way, but his harsh profile hadn't softened. Nevertheless, he'd given her an opening.

"They said you'd taken care of my horses," she dared quietly.

"They're in my barn. Your other things are up in one of the bedrooms by now."

"Thank you."

The brief conversation had an eerily normal sound, but Wes's level tone of voice when he radiated such anger deepened her new wariness of him.

"I need to explain today," she offered softly.

"You're gonna *volunteer* information?" He turned his head and gave her a glittering look that conveyed mock surprise.

The bite of sarcasm made her feel a little hopeless. "And I owe you an apology."

Something flickered in his dark gaze and he faced forward to glare out the windshield. "I'll want to hear all of it, and I'll want the truth."

He couldn't have made it clearer that he doubted her honesty. After all the things he'd gotten her to admit to him or tell about herself, this was a signal that her initial evasions had undermined her credibility with him.

And if that wasn't bad enough, she remembered what he'd said to her in the den two days ago when he'd decided to marry her. *You'll not shame me.* Then, he'd been talking about marrying a woman dressed as a cowhand.

Today, his wife of two days had got herself arrested. It might not be possible to calculate the extent of the shame that had caused a proud man like Wes. And it wasn't possible for Hallie to feel more guilt or regret for it.

Supper was tense. Wes barely spoke to her or looked her way, focusing on his meal with single-minded determination. Hallie forced herself to eat and she watched as he cut into his steak with strong, efficient movements, as he methodically cleared his plate. The vague impression of relentlessness and suppressed violence made mincemeat of her nerves.

Her mind repeated the hospital scene when she'd looked into her grandfather's eyes and suddenly saw him as he was, finally got the full impression of the evil that had twisted his brain. She couldn't help that her perceptions of Wes had also been shaken. The kindness she'd sensed in him, the compassion and decency and goodness, his affection toward his sister—had those been real? Or was she about to find out that they were merely a veneer?

She remembered the ruthless words he'd said to her the night of their wedding when he'd become suspicious of her. *It won't matter that you're my wife. You mean nothing to me.* Hallie's churning stomach threatened to rebel.

Her sudden distress made her set down her fork and pluck her napkin from her lap as she rose. She left the dining room at a dignified pace she hoped concealed her growing illness. She was so shaky by the time she'd gone upstairs that she was afraid she couldn't make it to the master bath.

For a woman who'd survived the upsets in her life with strength and resilience, it was shocking to feel so ragged and shaken and limp. She sat down on the edge of the bathtub and leaned her shoulder and head against the cool tile, waiting for the nausea to calm.

The memory of what had happened at the hospital invaded her thoughts. She'd struggled all day not to relive it, but she was suddenly too weak to blot out those appalling moments at her grandfather's bedside.

She'd waited her whole life for some sign of acceptance from Hank, to have a value to him beyond the low-ranking employee he rarely acknowledged, to win a bit of praise, to at last be blessed with some show of affection, however small.

Today she'd realized her wildest dreams. She'd gotten it all, everything she'd hungered for, everything she'd wanted. But it had all been based on the cunning and guile Hank believed of her, rewards for the wrong he believed she'd done and the wrong he hoped to accomplish through her marriage to Wes. Even the fact that she'd gone behind his back to marry with the hope he'd never find out had marked her as a Corbett in Hank's eyes.

That was the moment she became too ill to hold back.

CHAPTER SEVEN

WES reached the top of the stairs. He'd come after Hallie because it was time to have this out; he'd wanted to hear the details about how she'd got herself arrested, but not until his anger had mellowed and they'd both had something to eat.

She'd left the table before she'd eaten much, and gone upstairs. He'd assumed she'd go to his bedroom, but now it seemed odd that she'd do that. For a woman like Hallie, the bedroom suggested an intimacy they both knew she couldn't handle. Unless she'd thought to delay things by going to bed early.

Hallie was sitting on the edge of the bathtub when she heard Wes enter the bedroom. She felt wrung out. The last thing she wanted to deal with was a confrontation with him, but it was inevitable. Hallie straightened and forced herself to stand. She didn't want Wes to see her like this. Because they were at odds, she didn't want to chance that he'd think she was putting on a pitiful act to get him to back down.

She glanced into the big mirror over the sink. She rubbed her fingers roughly against her cheeks to coax some color back into them, then opened a drawer for toothpaste.

"Halona?"

Wes's deep voice on the other side of the door gave her no hint of his mood. The nausea had passed, and she was suddenly too exhausted to be afraid of him. The heavy lethargy that was pulling her down also provided an increasing apathy that she welcomed.

"I'll be out in a minute," she called, then got a glass and twisted on the tap. By the time she'd freshened up, her uneasiness had revived and panic fluttered in her middle. Whatever happened with Wes now, it would be over soon. She turned toward the door and opened it.

She didn't know if she were more relieved or on guard when she walked out of the bathroom to see Wes half-sitting, half-lying on the bed, his back against the headboard and his long legs stretched out on the coverlet. His folded hands rested casually on his middle, but he watched her with an intensity that made her shutter her expression.

He'd never looked so ruggedly handsome. His unsmiling features were so primitively male, so distinctively cut and so deeply appealing that she couldn't help being affected. His dark gaze was sharp on her face, but some of the anger about him had eased.

"You all right?"

"I'm fine." She came to a halt halfway between the path from the bathroom and the side of the bed. He didn't keep her waiting.

"So, do I have it right? You and Candice got into a fight at the hospital, she ordered you to get your things off the ranch and you borrowed a Four C's pickup and trailer to do it?"

He'd used the word "borrowed" and given it an emphasis that suggested he thought she'd done it without permission, that she'd provoked Candice on purpose and brought the arrest on herself. She *had* brought the arrest on herself, but it'd been unintentional.

"You brought in my ownership papers, so you know the horses were mine along with the other things in the trailer," she reminded him quietly. "What sense would it make for me to use a pickup and stock trailer without her permission, when I know Candice is hot to get at me?"

"Uh-huh. So, *knowing Candice is hot to get you,* you ignored the fact that I could have provided you with a truck and trailer and made sure you had ownership papers on you before you set foot on Four C's," he said, his low voice level. "And, *knowing Candice is hot to get you,* you walked right into a neat little piece of work without a whisper of caution. Explain to me, Halona, just how beneficial it is for you to *know* about Candice? Unless you meant to provoke her."

He hadn't raised his voice but her ears pounded with the accusation as if he had. He'd seemed to read her so easily, but he was staring at her now as if they'd never met. She'd made a stupid mistake, and though she'd been upset and scattered at the time, she should have known better. Clearly, Wes meant to upbraid her for it.

Because his pride had taken a blow, she wasn't certain he could be reasonable. The kindness and understanding she'd thought he had must have been a veneer after all. Pretending them had made her easier to control, but now that she'd slipped up, he wouldn't bother. She couldn't help the bitterness she felt.

"You seem to have it all figured out, Wes. I don't know what I can add." She hesitated when she saw the disturbing flare of anger in his dark eyes, then forced herself to go on. "What happens now?"

"What happens now is that you explain yourself. And you finally wise up about Candice."

Her gaze shied from his harshness. Hallie lifted her hands and took hold of the set of rings. She felt a spasm of pain as she pulled them off. They glittered in her palm and she couldn't seem to take her eyes off them. She gritted her teeth and looked over at Wes.

"What difference could it make now?" She tossed the unsoldered set of rings to him. His big hand came up and reflexively caught the engagement ring, but the wedding band missed his hand and flew past him to bounce lightly on the coverlet. His gaze broke contact with hers long enough to retrieve it. She went on.

"The only thing we need to discuss is whether you'll let me use a guest bedroom tonight so I can move out tomorrow. Unless you'd rather I got a motel room right away."

Wes's head snapped back to her and she felt the blunt concussion of his anger. Temper blazed high in his eyes and his expression went so hard that she felt a sick stab of terror.

Now she'd see Wes Lansing unmasked. Now he'd reveal the brutality he'd hidden. She relived the shock of what she'd seen in her grandfather that day, how the evil in him had fully shown itself. Hallie realized dimly that she'd wanted to put Wes to the test. As

terrified as she was of what he'd reveal, she'd needed
to see it now while she was prepared for it.

In the next second, Wes vaulted off the bed and
reached her in one long stride. It had happened so fast
that she could only fall back a step and put up her
hands to ward him off.

"You'd rather throw these rings at me and hare off
to a motel than explain what happened today," he
concluded, his low voice a growl.

Hallie flinched at his vehemence and eased further
back. "Yes."

The hard look he was giving her, the way he
loomed over her with every line of his big body rigid
and intimidating, made her brace herself. It was then
that she saw the flicker in his dark eyes, some faint
hint of perception.

"All right, Halona. Run."

It took her a moment to register the words and a
moment more to turn from him and walk to the door
on legs that didn't feel coordinated. His voice froze
her when her fingers touched the doorknob.

"But don't you dare let me believe something
that's not true. If I've got it wrong about today, correct me."

A crush of emotion drove the air from her lungs
and she began to shiver uncontrollably. Gray dots
swirled in the air between her eyes and the door. Only
a determined effort to breathe made them fade.

"I'm not sure I can...." She gritted her teeth, desperate to keep from falling apart. She didn't know
what was worse, what had happened with Hank and
her arrest, or the fact that Wes was angry and wanted

her to recount it all when she'd handled it all so incompetently.

The silence stretched. She was so attuned to the big male body halfway across the room behind her that she could feel it when his anger eased and began to fade.

Wes released a long breath. "I forget what it means to you to be a Corbett," he said quietly, "that you've got a history with them that I don't, that there are emotions involved that might confuse things."

Hallie stared blindly at the door, affected by the calm in his voice, the patience, his understanding.

"It's important to me to know what happened. I don't want these rings to gather dust someplace if there was no reason for them to come off."

Hallie lifted her hand and rested her fingers on the smooth wood of the door. He was giving her a chance; he *wanted* to give her a chance. She pressed her palm against the wood, so overwhelmed with gratitude and longing that she doubted she could speak.

She heard his footsteps behind her the second before his big hands settled on her shoulders. When she jerked, his fingers tightened.

"The bedroom is the place for intimacy, for sharing secrets, for learning to let someone see who you are in a way you don't show the world. Tell me about today, Halona. Make me understand."

Hallie literally couldn't get a word past the huge knot in her throat. She loved it when he spoke gently to her like this. On the heels of that realization, it came to her that she might also love him. How else could she explain the tender confusion of emotion he made her feel?

Wes's fingers and thumbs massaged gently and the sparkling pleasure that poured over her took some of the stiffness from her body. His hands slid to her upper arms.

"Come sit down."

His hands fell away. Hallie turned and walked over to sit on one of the overstuffed chairs at the side of the room. Wes hunkered down in front of her and reached for her left boot.

A little shocked, her first impulse was to rise, but Wes was too close. One of his hands gripped the back of her calf and the other gripped the heel to smoothly pull her boot off.

"Something else you need to learn about me is that I've got a temper. Which might be why I started this wrong. I'm sorry. I'd like to do it better this time." He set her boot aside, eased her foot down, then reached for her other ankle.

Hallie could only stare, mesmerized by the calm intensity in his dark eyes, nearly hypnotized by the casual way he removed her boots. He did it as if this was a regular ritual between them, a demonstration of caring. And he'd apologized. He grew even taller in her estimation.

He set her foot down, placed the second boot beside the other, but stayed hunkered down in front of her. He rested a muscled forearm on a bowed thigh and braced his other hand on the chair cushion beside her knee.

"If it helps to know it, that bogus arrest means

nothing to me beyond the upset it caused you. But I'm mad as hell because you didn't call me for help when you were in trouble. It made me doubt you, and I don't want to doubt my wife.''

Hallie looked away from him. He made her heart ache and he sharpened her hunger to be loved. And every time he did something kind for her or talked to her as if she meant something to him, he let her glimpse the ideal man to love.

But if he was the ideal man, he deserved to have his ideal woman. She wasn't good enough for him and though he'd surely see that very soon, she suddenly didn't want it to happen because of the mistakes she'd made today.

"Candice was upset," she began, then gave Wes a word-for-word repeat of everything she and Candice had said to each other, including the insult she wasn't proud of. "I believed her threat about my horses. She gave me permission to use a pickup and trailer, so I thought I could handle it myself." She made herself look at him. "I wasn't thinking. I didn't mean to do anything that would bring shame on you or the Lansing name. I'm sorry.''

"The Lansing name won't be hurt. When it gets around, Candice will be the one who's muddied." He reached over to take her hand, and he studied her face as relief eased over her. "What happened with Hank to set Candice off?''

Hallie tried to tell him. The long moments it took to start were so filled with hurt and emotion that she wasn't certain she could manage it. She couldn't look at him. Wes rubbed his thumb over the back of her hand and waited.

Hallie began slowly. When she finished, she took a shaky breath, amazed that telling him all of it had taken a heaviness off her heart. For the first time in her life, she felt as if she was sharing a burden with someone who could easily bear the weight.

She looked at Wes and said with quiet sincerity, "I'd never be part of any plan to harm you or anything you own."

But she still saw Hank as a powerful man. The combination of power and evil intent worried her. The fact that Hank wouldn't care about legalities or fair play made her anxiety that much worse. "Is there any way you know that he can use me to hurt you?"

Wes's somber gaze searched hers. "Does your loyalty still belong to me, Halona?"

The question was gentle, but she felt a stab of pain. "Yes."

"Then Hank Corbett can't hurt me.

His confidence in that—in her—overwhelmed her, but it also made her feel guilty. Ironically, her loyalty to Wes might deny him what he'd married her to get.

"When Hank realizes he can't use me, he'll write me out of the Will." She impulsively put her free hand over the back of his. "And I'm sorry for that. I wanted you to have the homestead."

Wes's hand tightened on hers. "It won't be the end of the world if I don't get it, Hallie. I've got thirty thousand acres of Texas and more money than I'll ever need. And a wife. Except for a house full of babies, I reckon I've got as much or more than any reasonable man can hope to have in this life.''

A wife. He'd listed that with everything else that made him feel content with his life. *Except for a house full of babies.* Such shocking words to say to her, especially after the others. Her heart was pounding with terror and excitement, so stirred up with longing that she couldn't allow herself to hope. There was a gallant generosity in Wes Lansing, so of course he'd say kind things. But as wonderful as they sounded, she couldn't let herself believe in them.

She pulled her hands from his and signaled that she was about to stand. Wes unbent his long legs and rose to give her room.

''If it's all right, I'd like to shower. I'm tired.'' She couldn't look straight at him. They'd resolved the problems of today, but now she needed to distance herself from him. He was saying too many wonderful things and they'd soon be sharing his bed.

Wes's neutral voice put her at ease. ''I've got a little book work, then I'll be back.''

Hallie nodded. She went to the big closet to collect her nightclothes before she started for the bathroom.

Hallie laid quietly in the dim bedroom as she listened to the shower run in the master bath. Confession was supposed to be good for the soul, and it must be, because when she'd laid her head down on her pillow that night, she'd felt more at peace. The traumatic events of that day had been aired, and something had been regained with Wes that she'd thought had been lost.

She tried not to think about the fact that he hadn't returned the rings. Perhaps she didn't deserve to have them back after she'd tossed them at him. Her conscience still squirmed at the memory.

It was a reminder that she was out of her element and floundering. She understood animals, she understood nature and she was competent with ranch work, but relationships were much more difficult. Especially her marriage to Wes. The fragile peace she'd achieved began to fade as worry seeped into her mind.

Were all the things Wes had said about *this* marriage and *his* wife as significant as he'd made them sound? Or had she imagined it? She knew she was vulnerable to talk like that, so she was afraid she might assign it a meaning Wes didn't intend. It distressed her that the things he'd said had made her craving for love that much more intense, and that he'd put notions in her head that defined her hunger more precisely than she wanted.

Hallie heard the shower go off and felt a rise of tension. It seemed as if a lifetime had passed since last night. Things had changed between them, but what would that mean tonight? What would Wes expect?

What if he expected nothing? What if he climbed into bed beside her, switched off the lamp, then turned away and went to sleep? She yearned for too much to not be hurt by that. On the other hand, wasn't hurt better than the anxiety she'd feel if he turned to her for the intimacy he'd expect from a wife?

For her, the mechanics of intimacy and sex were shadowy beyond the clinical facts presented in a high-school health class. She'd grown up on a ranch, so she'd seen animals mate. But animals acted on instinct and performed a biological function without the complication of human complexity or emotion.

She'd never been kissed before Wes had kissed her in the chapel. He'd kissed her later that night, but since then, nothing. She'd been such a beginner that he surely wouldn't expect more unless he first took time to educate her further. Relief trickled through her. Perhaps her kisses were so unimpressive that he wasn't interested in a tutorial. And if he wasn't interested in teaching her some skill at kissing, he probably wouldn't expect anything else from her.

So why was he saying things to her like *If it comes to that* regarding divorce? Why had he told her that he'd felt lust when she'd first gone to him, that it had influenced his willingness to bargain with her? Why would he want to stay married to a woman who didn't excite him sexually? Or a woman who never would?

Her speculations vanished the moment the bathroom door opened and Wes walked out. She closed her eyes, hoping he'd think she'd already fallen asleep. If he turned away then, it wouldn't be a rejection.

But, if he *was* interested, perhaps the fact that she seemed to be asleep would spare her the expectations he might have of a wife. Expectations she was terrified she couldn't fulfill.

Wes reached the other side of the bed and pulled down the coverlet and top sheet. The mattress gave with his weight as he got into bed and covered himself. But instead of switching off the light, he turned toward her and his big body settled a mere hand span from hers. She immediately felt the heat.

"Are you resting your eyes or faking it?" The amusement in his low voice let her know she hadn't fooled him.

Hallie opened her eyes and looked up into his strong features. He eased his arm around her and stroked her cheek with the back of a big knuckle. She couldn't help that her lashes flickered down at the pleasure his touch set off.

"All this time, we've lived on opposite sides of a fence," he said quietly, "the descendants of a bloody feud, and never knew, never suspected, that we'd be lying here together as husband and wife."

Hallie looked up into his dark gaze and his knuckle stilled on her cheek. He moved his hand and held up his fingers. He wore her rings on his pinkie finger. Because the rings were so small and his finger was so large, the rings fit snugly just past the cuticle of his blunt fingernail. He slipped them off, then reached for her left hand to slide them on her ring finger.

"Unless you wear these on a chain around your neck when you're working, I don't want you to take them off."

The dictate wasn't spoken harshly, and though it was an unmistakable order from a man who aimed to get his way all the time, Hallie didn't resist as the rings went on. She held her hand up to see them glitter and flash in the lamplight and felt as comforted as she felt obligated.

Why was she so relieved to have the rings back?

Was she so desperate to belong to a man? Her gaze shifted to Wes and she suddenly knew that he might be the only man she'd ever want to belong to. She couldn't help the terror of that.

Wes leaned down and she felt her breath go shallow in anticipation. The touch of his strong mouth on hers was tentative at first, then teasing. He enticed her to respond, then gave her the gentle reward of damp tongue strokes and tender bites when she did. Hallie's breath caught at each new thing, and she was suddenly helpless to keep from reaching up to wrap her arms around him.

His hard, bare skin was hot to the touch. Her fingers went wild, as if they had a compulsive mind of their own and were starved to explore the resilient texture of smooth male flesh over unyielding muscle and sinew and bone.

More of his weight crushed down on her and her body welcomed it. She felt his fingers graze her throat, then tug at the high buttons of her nightgown. She shivered when his broad palm skimmed her chest to smooth away the soft fabric, but her body jerked when his hand closed over her bare breast.

Wes increased the tender fervency of his kisses until she melted. By the time his mouth slid off hers and he kissed his way down to her breast, she was mindless. His hot mouth closed over the tip and drew gently. She couldn't help her gasp or the fact that her fingers combed shakily into his thick hair to urge him on.

Her body was no longer hers, it was Wes's, and he orchestrated every move, every sharp gasp and every low sound of raw pleasure it made. Because he overwhelmed her with heart-staggering delights, her brain ceased to function on anything but an instinctive level. Her fears of intimacy had been skillfully silenced, and there was no place for caution in her pleasure-drugged mind.

The craving to meld with Wes, to find some way to satisfy the desperate hungers of these escalating pleasures, removed every restraint. Even when she felt a spasm of pain, Hallie was so senseless with the unimagined joys of sexual intimacy and the soul-deep sense of connection to Wes that the pain barely registered.

Wes should have allowed Hallie to remain a virgin. Her life had been turned upside down, and she was still reeling from the changes while she tried to find her footing. Today had been traumatic for her. Even without her reclusive history, it would have been too soon for sexual intimacy.

He prided himself on his sexual self-control, but the few kisses that he'd hoped would bring Hallie closer to him had instead rapidly escalated to the point of no return. He'd overwhelmed her and she'd not had the experience to resist him, much less push him back from the edge.

A woman who'd been bullied and run over all her life would hate to have her sexual vulnerabilities exposed and taken advantage of. Which was what he'd done. He'd kissed his way past her resistance and once he was there, he'd lost his head and aimed straight for the deep need to be loved that she fought so hard to hide.

The primitive part of him had wanted to do that, had wanted to do it right away, to somehow mark her as his and bind her to him. She'd pledged her loyalty to him, but her bond to the Corbetts was still strong. Hank and Candice were cunning enough to confuse her loyalties despite what they'd done to her today.

Consummating this marriage had upped the emotional ante for them both, but it would have even more meaning for a woman who'd had so little affection that whatever she got was precious. And if nothing else, Halona Lansing now had a more compelling connection to him, one that might make it easier to choose if the Corbetts ever put her to the test.

He should have allowed Hallie to remain a virgin, but as Wes laid there in the dark with her sleep-weighted body half over his, he remembered what she'd made him feel and how perfectly she'd responded to him. And because the tantalizing memory was so fresh and so vivid, the primitive part of his psyche was fiercely glad he hadn't spared her.

CHAPTER EIGHT

THAT next morning, they slept until after seven a.m. Hallie woke first. Once she got over the shock of finding herself clinging to Wes, she realized that he clung to her, his arm heavy and tight around her as if he meant to keep her there. His rugged face was relaxed. His jaw was heavily shadowed, in need of a shave, and she recalled the unexpected pleasure of watching him do it the morning before.

Pleasure. It was a word she'd associated with ice water on a sweltering day, or those first moments at night when she laid down on her bed and felt her aching body relax muscle by muscle into the clean comfort of fresh cotton sheets. She'd always enjoyed the pleasure of riding a good horse who performed well, the pleasure of a cool, quiet dawn and the pleasure of a spectacular sunset on a warm summer evening.

But the pleasure of a man—the pleasure of *this* man—made the modest pleasures of her life seem like splinters and fragments of the pleasures that could be: deep pleasures, sensual pleasures, pleasures so shatteringly perfect and drenched with meaning that thinking about her first experiences of them overwhelmed her. Then there was the new list of uncomplicated pleasures: like watching Wes shave, touching his body, watching the way he moved, lying next to him, listening to the bourbon dark sound of his voice...

How would she live without the pleasure of this man? How could she give him up?

She'd known from the first that this marriage couldn't last. It would have no reason to go on once the Will was read and Hank's wishes were revealed. Was it possible that even after Wes had so thoroughly initiated her into the act of lovemaking that he could let her go, or worse, send her away?

Hallie couldn't help that she rubbed her cheek on the hard contours of Wes's wide chest like a stray kitten begging for a warm place to stay. The mental picture sent shards of ice through her veins and she stopped the motion.

She couldn't, however, stop the hungry exploration of his skin. Her fingers moved lazily in small circles and sensual lines on his chest, learning and absorbing the textures and contrasts of hair-studded skin and smooth warm flesh. She indulged in the luxury of human touch in a way she'd rarely been permitted or had allowed herself.

But only because Wes was still asleep. When he awakened, she'd retreat. She didn't relish facing him those first moments with the memory of last night between them. What would he be like today? Had something changed for him, or would he be the same?

She was changed. Irrevocably. Pride dictated that she not show him how much he'd affected her, or what last night had done. And she couldn't allow herself to show any of the deep affection she felt for him now, affection that made her ache to touch and soothe

and tantalize him. Affection that made her want to
learn everything she could about him and be his com-
panion, his mate. To share his life, to make it better
somehow, maybe to grant his wishes, however simple
or demanding, but mainly, to have the joy of pleasing
him.

The foolishness of her thoughts was proof of her
ignorance and naïveté. What on earth could a woman
like her give a man like Wes Lansing? She was ignorant of so much, she knew how to do so few things
that a man like him might require of a wife. Wes
Lansing was too smart and accomplished and suc-
cessful to find happiness with a socially inexperienced
woman who carried more emotional liabilities than
most men would care to bother with. What more
could she be to him than a burden?

Hallie was so distracted by her dismal thoughts that
when Wes's hand settled over hers, she was startled.

"Don't stop." Wes's voice was gravelly from
sleep and he pressed down on her hand to keep it on
his chest. "On second thought…" His fingers gently
plucked her hand off his skin and held it up. The ring
set glimmered. "You have beautiful hands, Halona. I
like to look at them."

The compliment sent an uneasy flush through her.
"They're a little beat up and callused," she said quietly.

Wes inspected her hand as if looking for flaws.
"Three small scars gone white, but this isn't an idle
hand. I see competence and sensitivity. You have interesting hands that move with an elegant style that
draws the eye." He turned his head to look at her as

his thumb stroked her palm. "Gentle hands that soothe and excite. Damn near magic."

His mouth quirked in a half-smile. "A poet could make that sound fancy."

Hallie's heart was squeezing madly. She couldn't seem to stop herself from pulling her hand from his to put her palm against his hard jaw in a rush of feeling so strong that her eyes stung with it.

The gruff words, "Good morning, wife," were barely out before he pulled her up so her face was over his. He meant to kiss her, she could read the intent in his dark eyes. "Kiss me, Halona."

Self-consciousness overwhelmed her. "M-morning mouth."

Wes's burst of laughter startled a wary smile from her. "Don't tell me I've been burdened with a per-snickety wife!"

Hallie suddenly found herself flipped onto her back with Wes hovering over her.

"So my breath stinks, huh?"

Hallie shook her head, appalled. She got out a hasty, "No-mi—" just as Wes tickled her sides. The giggle slipped out then hitched on a gasp of surprise and they both went still. Wes's gaze sharpened on her face. Discovery flared in his dark eyes and a slow grin curved his strong mouth.

"Persnickety *and* ticklish. Helluva combination."

His big fingers gently attacked her sides, sending her into giggles that were too spontaneous and freeing to suppress. After a helpless moment, Hallie tickled him back in self-defense, and both of them were soon laughing like children.

Until Wes's dark head swooped down and his lips sealed their laughter in their throats. The lightness between them switched instantly to need. Giggles turned to low moans of pleasure and hunger. Passion blotted out thoughts of anything else.

"You've blushed so much this morning, Halona, that I wonder if we should have your blood pressure checked."

Wes was sitting back with a second cup of coffee as they lingered after breakfast on the back veranda.

"We didn't scandalize Dora and Marie by having sex before breakfast," he informed her, his strong mouth curved in amusement when she colored again. His gaze sharpened on her warm cheeks as if he wanted to see how high her color would go. His dark eyes sparkled with devilment.

"Now, if we did it out here on the porch in full day while Marie was sweeping up and Dora was clearing the plates, *that* would be a scandal."

Wes was still in a playful mood and Hallie found that irresistible. *Wes* was irresistible. She couldn't help the wonder and delight of being the focus of his gentle teasing. Because it was so clearly affectionate, his attention warmed her and coaxed her heart closer to him. The sky had never seemed so blue or the sun so bright. She felt a happiness and contentment she'd never known and her insides ached with the sweetness of it.

"Remember those two-year-olds I mentioned?" he asked.

She welcomed the shift of conversation. Work was

more familiar to her than this overdose of contentment and emotion. She needed time to adjust and sort it out in her mind, to figure out what it all meant.

"I'd like you to have a look at them. I don't know what you like to do, but if you're interested in helping me start them and getting them finished, then they can sample a little work over the summer before they do it full time next year."

A smile sparkled in his eyes. "Unless you'd rather go to San Antonio to shop. Or run away with me to some isolated mountain cabin or tropical resort." His face went more serious. "And I mean that, Halona. I'll take you any place on this planet and do anything you want to do."

The words brought a fresh surge of emotion. He'd meant every word and she was powerfully affected.

Now his smile edged back. "The only rule is you've gotta sleep with me skin to skin."

Both his offer and the order—and she didn't doubt that he meant them both—caught her off guard. It must have shown on her face.

"It's nice to know I can take your breath away as quickly out of bed as I can in it." A suggestive smile that was pure male arrogance stretched over his mouth. "Gives me a thrill as big as Texas, darlin'."

Hallie's blush as she caught the hint went so high that Wes chuckled softly.

The day was unlike any Hallie had ever had. The fact that she spent every moment of it with Wes made it so. If there was a more attentive husband or one who was more patient and generous and affectionate, she couldn't imagine him.

She'd been grateful and pleased when she'd discovered that Wes shared her view of starting young horses using patience and gentle hands to win their trust, rather than trying to dominate them through pain and intimidation. But she'd never forget what he showed her once he'd had her choose the first young horse and he put it in a round, tube-rail corral.

"You ever read that Monte Roberts book about listening to horses?" he'd asked her. He saw the questioning look in her eyes. "I'll give it to you at supper. Meanwhile, I'll show you how he does it."

Hallie stood outside the rails and watched with fascination as Wes worked with the young horse. She strained to hear as he explained what he was doing in a calm voice that didn't startle the young animal.

She watched, enthralled as he demonstrated Advance and Retreat, as he decoded for her the equine behaviors and responses that she'd seen before but had never assigned such precise significance. It was a new language for her, a new method of communication between horse and man, and yet the form of communication wasn't new, Wes explained, horses had been speaking it all along.

For a woman who'd worked closely with horses her whole life yet had been ignorant of the depth and scope of the language of Equus, it was a revelation. Wes's demonstration opened her eyes to it, and she could only stare in wonder, when after little more than a half hour, the young horse calmly tolerated Wes's weight in the saddle and was walking around the circular corral as if it pleased him to do so.

Wes finished with the young horse and took a few minutes to rub his forehead and praise him before he handed the horse over to a stable hand. Hallie joined Wes for the walk to select a second horse. She eagerly asked, "Had that colt ever been handled before?"

Wes glanced at her as they walked. "Whatever handling they've had since they were weaned has been sparse. They've been in the pasture for four days, so whatever they've had during that time is all they've had lately, which isn't much."

"Will this method work with them all like that?" she asked next.

"In my experience, it works nearly every time. It gets trickier with a horse that's been mistreated and gone sour from abuse or poor handling."

They paused at the gate and Wes looked over at her. "You want to try it, or do you want to watch a while longer?"

Hallie had wanted to watch. Part of her was afraid it was too wonderful to be real. But as she watched Wes work three more young horses, she realized that something important was going on, something humane, something that might change forever the relationship between horses and humans.

She watched Wes give the last young horse an affectionate rub and speak gently to him. The admiration she felt for him soared. It amazed her now that she'd ever thought he might have a dark side or a potential for violence, and she felt guilty for doubting him.

Wes walked out of the corral and they started to the house for a late lunch. Dora had set the table and laid out a meal of pasta salads, sliced tomatoes and cold beef sandwiches before she'd left to go grocery shopping.

As they sat down at the kitchen table to eat, Hallie cautiously remarked, "I didn't see the morning paper."

Wes sent her a neutral look and passed her the plate of sandwiches. "Dora and Marie had orders to put the papers away."

Hallie's gaze streaked from his as her heart sank. "Then they printed the story about the arrest." It wasn't a question. She'd tried not to think about the possibility of it making the papers. Things had been so perfect today between her and Wes. Coming back to earth gave her a jolt. She tried to conceal her reaction, but her soft, "I'm sorry," gave her away. "Was it bad?" She looked over at him as she handed back the sandwich plate.

"Once you get past the headline, it was a fair account. It mentioned the bad blood between our families, but it reported that the charges had been dropped." A faint smile curved his mouth. "And something I didn't know. Charges are being considered against Candice. I doubt it'll come to that, but she'll think twice before she pulls another stunt like that one."

He studied her pale face a moment. "You have to remember that you're a mystery, Halona. Not many people know anything about you. They already have a negative opinion of the rest of the Corbetts, so the fact that you came under attack from Candice will automatically make you the good guy. Don't feel bad about this.''

Hallie stared over at him, afraid to believe he was this pragmatic about it. "What about you? Even though the charges were dropped, I was still arrested.''

Wes leaned back. "If it had been the simple cat-fight I originally thought it was, I'd be upset. But there's nothing simple about the history between you and Candice. I think you've lived with her so long that you don't see how dangerous she is.'' He paused, then added, "Don't let her catch you again without witnesses.'' His dark gaze went cool, underscoring how seriously he meant that.

Perhaps she should have resented his dictate, but she didn't want a repeat of yesterday any more than he did. It troubled her to know he thought she might be blind to Candice, and maybe she was. She'd weathered her cousin's petty torments so often that she wasn't fazed by most of them.

She hadn't seen yesterday coming and she still felt stupid for that. But in spite of Wes's reassurances, she couldn't believe that people would automatically think she was the good guy. If they did, it would have more to do with the fact that she was Wes Lansing's wife. Which was all the more reason to avoid anything else that might tarnish his name.

The insecurities she'd had her whole life stirred. Wes Lansing's wife ought to be worthy of his name, worthy of *him,* and she was afraid she wasn't.

The telephone rang and Marie must have picked it

up on the second ring on another extension, because she appeared at the kitchen door moments later.

"Miz Hallie? That was Mr. Corbett. I told him you were having lunch, so he wants you to call him when you can."

Hallie was surprised. "Thank you, Marie."

"You can use the phone in the den for privacy," Wes told her. Hallie toyed uneasily with the sandwich half she'd selected, then set it down.

"I'm not sure I want to."

"Why not?"

"Something's wrong. Hank always has someone else call." And never in her memory had he ever sought her out himself. If she wasn't available by phone, he sent someone to get her.

"He's probably seen the newspaper." Wes clearly disapproved. "You'd think Candice would try to shield a man in his condition from potential upsets."

"Candice is fighting for Four C's now," she said grimly. "And I'm not sure she really believes Hank will die."

Wes gave her a thoughtful look. "Is it possible Hank took exception to what she did yesterday? Could Candice have got herself in trouble with him?"

"Hank's only criticism of Candice is that she doesn't love Four C's," she said, then shrugged. "If he praised me for marrying you to get it, surely he'd also approve of what Candice did to me. She might not love Four C's, but she'll fight to get it."

Wes seemed to consider that. "It's not the same. What Candice pulled with that arrest didn't affect whether she'd get the ranch or not. It was a jealous payback. You married behind Hank's back to thwart his Will and guarantee Four C's.''

"And a marriage wasn't a public embarrassment," she concluded as she saw his point, "but the arrest of a Corbett was."

Wes's mouth relaxed into the hint of a smile. "The old man might be worried that Candice fouled up his plans. If he truly means to use you, the last thing he'd want is for something to jeopardize your relationship with me or to make you less inclined to let him influence you." He raised his dark brows as if asking her a question. "You might be in a more favorable position with Hank than you could have foreseen."

Hallie felt a spasm of intuition that made her deeply uneasy. "How?"

"Hank could be anxious to make it up to you. But the downside of that is that whatever he does is guaranteed to make Candice jealous." His face went somber. "And that means, like it or not, you don't step one inch off this ranch without me. Particularly if he tries to use his Will to manipulate her like he did you. About that time, Candice would be capable of just about anything."

Hallie looked away, her mind racing through memory after memory as she mentally tested ideas about the potential of "just about anything."

Wes's voice was quiet. "You realize, don't you, that Candice is sick. That if she hadn't made you a target for her venom all these years, she would have directed it at someone else. It's not because you deserved it or there was anything wrong with you."

His kindness was another indication of the man he

was, but Hallie had to disagree. "I should have stood up to them years ago."

"How?" His skeptical tone made her look at him. "You were a kid beholden to a reluctant relative for a home. If you'd bucked Candice too hard, you would have been turned over to some government agency."

Hallie shook her head. "I could have left when I turned eighteen."

"But by then, you loved the ranch. And you told me yourself that you couldn't walk away and let Candice get that, too. Staying gave you a chance for *some* justice."

"A chance," she said with quiet bitterness. "It was a good thing we didn't go into a casino when we were in Las Vegas. I might have found out for sure that I'm a compulsive gambler. Only the worst kind: the kind who hardly ever wins, but keeps pulling on that one-armed bandit like some demented robot."

"That's too harsh, Halona," he said sternly. "If you love Four C's as much as I love Red Thorn, you'd have put up with just about anything to stay on and bide your time."

Hallie put her napkin on the table and gripped it shakily. Everything Wes said to her was generous. Comforting. He understood her and he understood the family she'd grown up with in ways that she'd been too close to fully grasp.

His lack of criticism was both welcome and undeserved. She'd helped make her life the way it was, and she couldn't be as magnanimous with herself. Anyone with a better sense of self-preservation would have run far and fast to escape the Corbetts. She'd been as much a part of that sick dynamic as Hank or Candice. A handful of days away from them and exposed to Wes's vastly different worldview made that brutally clear.

"Halona?"

She forced back the confused emotions that fought for dominance and looked over at him. "Whether I call Hank back or not isn't entirely my choice. It's more than simply risking Hank's anger at me. It's also your choice because of the homestead."

Wes shook his head. "I told you, I've already got more than I'll ever need, so that homestead's only worth so much. Don't let it figure into what you think you need to do."

Hallie stared at him, searching for even a hint that he was simply being gallant. She couldn't help the twist of lips that passed for a smile. "For days I've made choices and taken actions that haven't gone exactly the way I planned." Her sharp sense of failure and incompetence made it possible to confess that.

"Maybe some of those were choices no one should have put in front of you, Halona. Not even me." His quiet words blunted the defeat she felt. "Maybe this time when he snaps his fingers, you can consider letting him wait for a reaction. At least until you eat a meal."

Hallie looked away before the aching blur in her eyes could give her away. She'd stepped into a new world when she'd walked into Wes's house a few days ago. It still confused her and she was afraid she'd never been good enough to stay, but the calm and sanity of it—of its owner—gave her such a sense of safety and peace that she never wanted to leave.

Hallie ended up calling the hospital to leave a message for Hank that she'd call him later. If Wes was right and Hank was worried about things in the wake of her arrest, then that might mean she had a bit of power.

And though she didn't necessarily want power, it made sense to her that if she sent the signal that she was no longer at Hank's beck and call, he might worry about it. Perhaps there'd be a smidgen of respect.

If Wes's take on the situation was wrong, she'd have lost nothing. She'd made another decision, and though she was wary of it going awry, she accepted the potential.

It actually felt better to make Hank wait than to fall all over herself to return his call. She hoped he realized that she'd meant to rebuff his first personal summons, and that he realized the significance, when for her first time, *she'd* been the one to send a message through a third party.

Hallie and Wes elected to avoid the extreme heat of the afternoon and stay at the house. Hallie asked for the newspaper, and when Wes handed it over, she saw for herself that the article hadn't been written to damage her.

It gave a fair account and kept the record straight. Candice did indeed come off looking in the wrong. Most people would resent a wealthy woman using the influence of her name to harass someone else, even if the person targeted was a member of the same family.

When she finished with the paper, Wes started to show her the computer programs he used for record keeping. Her immediate confession, that she'd never used a computer, made him spend the afternoon teaching the basics first, then instructing her on a tour of the Internet. He showed her some game software and the two of them played computer games.

Hallie lost track of time and was a little shocked when Dora came in to call them to supper. She finally decided not to call Hank at all, but to instead see him during regular visiting hours that evening.

Later, with every mile toward town, her tension went higher. But this time, Wes's steady presence gave her a confidence she'd never felt before.

"Did Lansing take it bad?" From the look on Hank's pale face, he was worried about that.

Hallie's soft, "What do you think?" was as much a small manipulation as it was a concealment. She hoped to discourage Hank from thinking he could get at Wes through her, but she didn't want a confrontation that would upset him. He wasn't looking as well as he had the day before. The gray cast to his skin had returned and he was again on oxygen.

If she was careful, he might realize that the potential advantages of her marriage to Wes had been lost to him. He might even realize they'd never been a possibility. She braced herself for the moment he would see it and discard her as useless.

"D'you 'spose Lansing would think my personal apology is worth anything?"

Hallie knew that Hank would intend any apology as a way to get on Wes's good side, to draw him in and make him let down his guard. Hank had no concept of the savvy, perceptive man he wanted to hoodwink. Fierce pride roared up at the thought.

All at once she saw something else about the tyrant who'd bullied and intimidated her all her life. Compared to Wes, Hank was a small-minded, pitiful man, so spiritually bankrupt and twisted with selfishness that he'd thoroughly deluded himself. Hank Corbett had never seemed so wretched. The fact that he was totally blind to it sent a shiver through her.

Hank's patience was nonexistent. "Did you hear me? I asked if you thought my apology is worth anything to Lansing."

Hallie watched him calmly, moved by the soulless futility of her grandfather's life, but too scarred by it to let him get away with everything, in spite of how near death he might be.

"It's interesting that you'd worry so much about apologizing to Wes," she said quietly. "You and I know you wouldn't really mean it. But will you apologize to me? You haven't offered me an apology yet, you haven't even hinted at one. Are you so sure of me? Or does pride keep you from stooping that low?"

Hank stared at her as if he'd gone blank. Then he seemed to recover. "I had nothing to do with what Candice did to you." His cough sounded distinctly uncomfortable and he was studying her as if he was trying to decide if he needed to do something to placate her. It was clear that he didn't want to waste much effort on her. Which she'd already known.

Hallie forced a slight smile. "If you're too innocent to owe me an apology, why would you owe one to Wes?" She made herself glance at the clock on his bed table as the silence stretched. "Wes didn't expect me to be here long. I shouldn't keep him waiting." She started to turn, but Hank's words made her hesitate.

"You gonna give your granddaddy a good-night kiss?"

The heartless calculation of that repelled her. She gave him a somber look and voiced a soft, "No." She saw the baffled flash in his eyes, but turned and walked out of his room with a dignity that felt effortless.

Once she was out the door, her gaze sought Wes, who leaned against the opposite wall a little down the hall. When he saw her, he straightened and waited for her to reach him, searching her stoic expression the whole time.

Neither spoke as he slid an arm around her waist and pulled her against his side. Hallie welcomed the strength of his body and felt renewed by it.

"You all right?"

"I'm fine," she told him, then realized with some surprise that she was. She'd maintained a dignity and emotional distance from Hank that she'd never before accomplished so easily. This time, seeing him as he was had been more a visual confirmation of what she'd always somehow known, rather than a shock.

And she'd stood up to him in a way she'd never

regret, perhaps in a way that might affect Hank more deeply and stay with him longer than if she'd done it harshly or in anger.

Though it had been small and low-key, it was a turning point. And whether anything ever changed in Hank, something had begun to change in her.

CHAPTER NINE

THE Texas evening was sultry, but uncommonly pleasant as Hallie and Wes walked together toward his car. Perhaps it was the deepening twilight and lingering heat, but the air had a heaviness to it that filled her lungs and seemed to flow languidly through her bloodstream. A warm tingle spread over her skin and she felt the soft ache of what could only be desire.

Suddenly it wasn't enough that she and Wes walked with an arm around each other's waists. It was all she could do to keep from turning into his arms for more, and she pressed her lips together to counter the craving to kiss him.

By the time he opened the car door for her and she got in, she was trembling. Anticipation made her feel restless and self-conscious. She'd managed to distract herself from the memory of Wes's lovemaking all day, but now that night was falling, the memories were so overwhelming that the eagerness she felt confused her. What was proper and natural, and what wasn't?

Hallie was aware of every move Wes made as he got in on the driver's side, closed the door, then slid the key into the ignition. She sensed his study of her tense profile, but she didn't let herself look at him. He might see something in her eyes that would give her away.

It made sense to her that her feelings were one-sided. Sexual feelings that were enthralling and novel for her were probably a lot less thrilling for a man as experienced as Wes. And because she was not at all sophisticated or confident of her appeal, she had to guard her every movement and glance.

"What do you want to do, Halona?"

The bourbon-deep sound of his voice sent a lazy stroke of heat through her that intensified everything. She caught the meaning behind his quiet question and knew instantly he was speaking to her on an intimate level. She couldn't help that she glanced his way briefly, partly to confirm her impression, partly in the hope of showing him a neutral expression.

Her softly stuttered, "N-nothing," spoiled it all and she felt a pang of faint horror.

Wes gave a slow smile. "A new bride with no thoughts about what she'd like to do?"

He was teasing her gently, inviting her to play. She felt a blush of excitement and desire as she stared at him, fascinated by the contrast of playful sexuality and bluntly rugged maleness he exuded.

She loved Wes deeply, especially for this. Every second she spent with him led her out of grim bondage toward a white light of peace and freedom she'd never believed in because she'd never known for sure they could exist. Instinct told her she was only beginning to sense the full impact Wes Lansing could have on her. If he let her stay in his life.

The overwhelming need to reach for him, to convince him let her stay, to somehow persuade him to love her, made her shake with the effort to hold herself back. She had to keep her feelings to herself, she could never risk his rejection by confessing them.

His smile faded slightly. "Move over here, Halona. I want to say something. Private." Her rounded eyes tracked the hand he dropped to the seat next to his thigh in a silent demonstration of how close he wanted her to sit. Her gaze jumped up to his and his intensity stole her breath.

"Come here, darlin'." That last was so low and husky that it found some invisible thread and tugged at her.

She slid hesitantly across the seat until she was next to him, angled to face him as much as the seat allowed. She braced her left hand on the back of the seat next to his arm and felt her other hand settle self-consciously on her thigh. He caught a lock of her dark hair to roll its silken texture between a heavily callused thumb and forefinger. His heavy-lidded eyes were mesmerizing and she was powerless to look away from them.

"A husband and wife have the right to each other's bodies," he said quietly, the deep timbre of his voice seductive. "That goes for kisses, embraces...and sex. I expect to touch you when I want, I expect you to touch me when you want. You'll always be welcome, Halona. I hope you'll always welcome me."

The utter seriousness of his somber words broke something in her. She was powerless to keep from putting her arms around him to hug him tightly. A flood of emotion surged up and she bit her lip savagely to counter the blinding sting in her eyes. Wes's hard arms crushed her and the kisses he pressed into her hair and on her shoulder seemed to burn through to her skin and tenderly mark her.

It took so long to get control of her emotions that she feared she couldn't do it. When at last she did, she drew back just enough to see his face. She searched his dark eyes, wary of letting herself fully believe that she'd see invitation and welcome in them, overwhelmed when she saw both and felt herself inch slowly toward him.

Her eyelashes closed the moment she touched her lips to his. The heady knowledge that she'd taken this first small initiative made her body pulse with excitement and traces of the fear that lingered. The need to taste his lips, to press her mouth to his and satisfy her hunger was too strong.

Guided by instinct, Hallie gave in to a passion and carnality she'd never suspected of herself. Her fervor increased as Wes responded with a lack of restraint that banished her fear and gave her such a deep feeling of acceptance that only their mutual breathlessness made her finally draw back.

Even then, she could manage only inches. And she couldn't keep from placing a few still-hungry kisses to his lean cheek and jaw. Wes's big hand came up to her face and it was reflex that made her turn her head to press an anxious kiss on his hard palm.

"I want you in bed," he said, his voice harsh with passion. "Now. Right now." He took a steadying breath that made his big body tremble. "Damned if I know why us Lansings settled Red Thorn so far from town."

Wes's cranky words startled a giggle out of her and

his gaze sharpened on her flushed face. "You think that's funny, huh?" The sparkle in his dark eyes and the faint curve of his strong mouth let her know that he was also amused by their predicament. "I'll give you something to giggle about, Mrs. Lansing," he vowed as he eased her away from him and reached to twist the ignition key.

He waited until she got her seat belt on, then sent her a smoldering look. "That's a promise."

Wes broke every speed limit on the way back to Red Thorn. They didn't make it to the top of the big staircase before Wes pulled her down to the steps and impatiently unbuttoned her blouse as he scattered voracious kisses to her tingling skin. Before she was completely exposed, he caught her up and carried her the rest of the way upstairs, kicking the door to their bedroom shut before he strode to the bed.

That night, they barely slept. And for the first time in more years than Hallie could remember, she wept. But she wasn't ashamed of the silent cascade of tears that welled from someplace deep inside her, because she knew the moment she felt them that they were an expression of joy.

And sometime in those early hours that next morning, when they finally feel deeply asleep in each other's arms, Hank Corbett passed away.

Hank Corbett's funeral wasn't as large as the family of a man of his wealth and business contacts should have expected, but it was large enough for appearances. It was clear to Hallie from the moment she'd walked into the biggest church in town that it wasn't affection or respect that filled the pews as much as it was business obligation and curiosity.

Because Hallie had insisted on it, she and Wes sat halfway back as members of the funeral crowd, not with Candice and a smattering of distant cousins who sat on the front row. She'd considered not attending the funeral at all, but whatever else Hank Corbett had been, he'd also been her grandfather.

Rather than share the funeral limousine with Candice, Hallie asked Wes to drive her to the private cemetery on Four C's for the graveside service. Again, she ignored the family seating across from the casket. She and Wes stood near the back of the crowd near her mother's gravestone, and she focused on her dim memories of the mother who'd died when Hallie was five.

Wes's arm tightened around her and she looked up at him. She'd worn one of the dresses she'd bought in Las Vegas. It was a cheery yellow with short sleeves and a nipped-in waistline with skirt gathers that flared stylishly to her knees. Hardly a mourning dress, but she'd dressed for Wes, not to indicate a level of grief she'd never feel.

Wes was ruggedly handsome in his black suit and pearl gray dress Stetson. His primitive, masculine look was overpowering, but the immaculate black suit gave the impression of a civilized man with a polish that equaled his natural ruggedness.

She loved him. Deeply and profoundly.

But he hadn't made love to her since Hank's death three days ago. He'd touched her often, they'd shared a few kisses, but what she'd initially taken as consideration because of Hank's death now seemed to be the first steps of a sexual distance that was the prelude to separation. Wes hadn't mentioned *his wife* or anything resembling the words *if* we divorce. And there'd been no hint of the words her heart ached to hear, *I love you*. She hadn't spoken them either.

Hallie couldn't help that she'd grown more remote. She'd taken long, solitary horseback rides on Red Thorn and tried to come to terms with Hank's death and her last stark impressions of the man who'd raised her, but she'd not spoken to Wes about them. Hallie suspected some of her renewed reclusiveness was a form of grief, but more a grief for the grandfather she'd never had than grief over the loss of Hank Corbett.

And during those many solitary hours, Hallie realized that the potential loss of Four C's meant nothing to her. Every moment that she felt Wes growing more distant taught her that there were far more wrenching pains to endure than the loss of a piece of real estate.

She'd known their marriage couldn't last. And even when it came to the divorce she feared, she'd leave Red Thorn a far different woman than the shy misfit who'd first walked into Wes's big house. She was grateful for that, but in the end, she knew it would never balance out the price of losing him.

Hank's Will was read the day after the funeral. Hallie dreaded it and was reluctant to attend, but Hank's lawyer had advised her that her presence was required.

At the large downtown law offices of Hank's attorney, Hallie and Wes were led into the lawyer's comfortable suite where they sat together on a leather sofa. Candice arrived after them and seated herself on a wing chair near the lawyer's desk.

Candice was dressed for deep mourning, from her stylish black dress, hosiery and accessories, to the fine black net veil that covered her face to the tip of her nose. She got out a black cotton handkerchief trimmed in black lace and sat gripping it.

Hallie had worn a simple white dress because it seemed the most businesslike of the dresses she'd bought in Las Vegas. No one could have missed the contrast between the cousins, and Hallie suspected that anyone who saw them together would get the visual impression of good vs. evil. Hallie hadn't been thinking about the contrast of that as much as her ongoing reluctance to give the impression that she mourned Hank.

Hallie noted that even with her cousin's beautiful face partly shadowed by the light veil, Candice had obviously been traumatized by Hank's death. The uncharacteristic tremor of her hands indicated how close she might be to breaking down. Hallie felt a touch of pity for her cousin before she sensed the raw hatred that burned out from behind the delicate veil.

Hank's lawyer organized the sheaf of papers on the desk before him and signaled he was ready to begin. The initial formalities were quickly out of the way, then the Will was read.

Hallie listened tensely as Hank's lawyer worked his way through the smaller bequests. The list was brief and Hank had not been generous. His lack of generosity seemed an indication that he would be just as stingy with her. Or worse.

The surprisingly sudden, "And to my granddaughter, Halona Corbett Lansing, I leave Four C's Ranch..." made her head go so light that a low roar began in her ears.

Candice's startled gasp made an impression the second before she felt the shock wave of her cousin's outrage. Wes's hand found hers and squeezed warmly. She turned stunned eyes to his and read the restrained congratulations in his dark gaze.

Hallie's attention snapped back to the lawyer when he read the directive that Hank had included in his Will: that Candice was to vacate Four C's ranch seven days from the date the Will was read, taking only her personal belongings and whatever household or personal items of Hank's that Hallie was willing to part with or sell to her.

The stunning harshness of that was a clear message of Hank's strong disapproval of Candice's scorn for the ranch he had prized as the Corbett family legacy.

Hallie's shocked gaze went to her cousin. Candice's mouth trembled, her skin had gone white, but she held her chin at a defiant angle. Her long red fingernails were dug into her handbag like talons, and the surge of hatred that rushed Hallie's way sent a quiver of anxiety through her.

Hank's lawyer paused a few moments and watched the cousins, waiting for Candice's silent enmity to ease before he continued the reading. It was obvious that more unpleasantness was coming for Candice, and Hallie's quiver of anxiety darkened to foreboding.

"...Halona Corbett Lansing also receives one-half of the total of my remaining assets," the lawyer went on.

"The remaining half of my assets, excluding my personal belongings and the household inventory on Four C's Ranch, I leave to my granddaughter, Candice Renee Corbett."

This time, Hallie couldn't look at her cousin. She was so numb as she realized the scope of her inheritance—and the fact that Candice had received so much less—that she sat in a dizzy haze that deepened as she realized the extent of the punishment Hank had leveled on his favorite granddaughter.

He must have rewritten his Will to punish Candice for the arrest, but Hallie didn't doubt that he'd also planned to change it once Candice had been chastened and brought back under his control. The irony was that he hadn't been able to control the moment of his death, so he'd run out of time before he could change his Will to again favor Candice.

Hank's lawyer rose and brought copies of the Will to Hallie and Candice. Once Hallie had signed a raft of legal documents, she left the office in a fog of shock and relief. She was shaky enough that she was glad of Wes's hand at her elbow. They'd reached the outer office before Candice caught up and stepped in front of them to block their exit. She moved so close that Hallie could see the blue fire in her cousin's eyes through the black netting of the veil.

"You'll never get Four C's—you have no right to it. No right!" The vicious hiss of her voice gave the impression of a venomous snake.

Wes's calm words carried a steely edge. "You have the option to contest the Will, Ms. Corbett. Notify your lawyer. Excuse us." He'd started to lead Hallie past her cousin, but Candice stepped to the side to again block their exit and continue her harassment.

"Look at yourself, Hallie," Candice said scornfully, untroubled that her rising voice attracted the attention of everyone waiting in the outer office. "Your marriage is a lie. Feminine clothes, makeup and the Lansing name can't change the fact that you're a piece of trash who could never get a decent man without a bribe."

Wes's voice was quiet, but harsh. "You're overwrought, Miz Corbett. You need to find someone to drive you home. Excuse us."

Wes ushered Hallie past her cousin, who turned to stalk out of the office after them. Hallie felt the burn of Candice's rage every step of the way until she and Wes got in his car and he drove away from the curb.

The ride to Red Thorn was silent, as if Wes understood that she needed the time to absorb it all. The joy of owning Four C's was so much less satisfying than she'd expected.

She'd had a right to Four C's by birth. She had a higher claim to it than Candice because she loved the ranch and Candice despised it. But Candice had been Hank's favorite. While Hallie had never believed her cousin should have Four C's, she'd always believed Candice had a right to everything else their grandfather owned. Particularly his personal effects, since they meant nothing to Hallie.

Troubled, Hallie glanced Wes's way. He caught the movement in his peripheral vision and looked over at her.

Her soft, "I think I need to find a lawyer," made him search her face briefly before his attention returned to the pavement ahead.

"You think Candice will fight you over the Will?"

"Before she tries, I'd like to make her an offer."

That got her a sharp look. "What kind of offer?"

"Everything but Four C's and six month's operating expenses."

Wes shook his head and faced forward. His profile was stern. "That extra capital is security, Hallie. You'll have inheritance taxes to pay. Four C's might be doing well now, but you can't predict the future. You've got employees who count on steady employment and the market is volatile." He sent her a perceptive glance. "She got to you, didn't she?"

This time, it was Hallie who glanced away from him to stare at the pavement ahead. Wes pushed on.

"Your whole life, they treated you like poor relation. *Worse* than poor relation. But the meek have inherited the lion's share of Corbett assets," he added, satisfaction in his voice as he roughly paraphrased the Bible verse.

He reached over and took her hand, prompting Hallie to look over at him. His gaze touched hers briefly before he faced forward. He gave her hand a gentle squeeze. "Don't rush into anything. You've had a lot coming your way these past few days, you've made a lot of changes. Take some time to let things settle, see what the future brings."

She couldn't help that she placed her free hand over the back of Wes's. Every touch of his was precious, particularly since they hadn't been intimate for days now. Maybe she shouldn't rush into any decision about Hank's Will. As she glanced at Wes's rugged profile, she had the sudden fear that there might be another message in his counsel.

See what the future brings. The words sent a light chill over her heart. It was prudent advice, but she was too unsure of herself to believe it was simple caution that had made him add that. Wes wasn't a cruel man. His natural inclination would be to look out for her best interests, even if they ended up going their separate ways. And if he'd already decided that would happen, he'd certainly believe she'd be better off with as much as Hank's Will had given her.

The knot in her throat expanded. She couldn't force herself to let go of his big hand until they pulled up in front of the main house on Red Thorn. Beth's car was parked at the end of the front walk. Hallie loosened her light grip on Wes's hand the precise moment he started to pull it away.

His gruff, "If she didn't bring that baby this time, she's in big trouble," was smiling and affectionate. Hallie forced a smile to fake a lighter mood.

She got out of the car before Wes could come around and open the door for her, but he caught up and they walked to the house. They were barely inside before Wes roared, "Where's my girl?"

Beth leaned out of the living room down the hall. Her urgent, "Shhh!" had no effect on the big rancher who pulled off his hat, tossed it toward a table near the door, then strode across the entry hall, the heels of his big boots ringing on the tile. Hallie followed at a more reserved pace.

Once they were all three in the living room, Wes walked straight to the white ruffled bassinet that had been placed near the sofa. Hallie looked on as Wes quickly removed his suit jacket and slung it over a nearby chair before he reached carefully into the bassinet.

Curiosity drew Hallie near enough to watch as Wes effortlessly lifted the sleeping baby, his huge hands managing the task with an ease that emphasized both his competence and the baby's tiny size.

At first, Hallie stared at Wes, watching closely as he settled the baby on his arm and turned fully toward her. But then she saw the sleeping child and she was suddenly blind to everything else.

Natalie Dade was a delicate, black-haired angel in her ruffled yellow sundress. Her tiny sandals were small enough to fit a doll and the yellow bow on top of her head couldn't have measured much more than an inch from fold to fold.

Hallie had rarely been around babies, but she'd never seen one this small. She didn't realize she'd continued to inch forward until the sound of Beth's voice broke the spell.

"I was hoping she'd sleep another hour, but if you clomp around in those big boots, she'll be awake sooner. And she gets cranky when she doesn't get her nap out."

Wes gave his sister a chiding look. "This little angel doesn't know how to be cranky. And," he added, a smug smile easing across his mouth, "she knows already that she'll never have to get cranky with her Uncle Wes to get what she wants."

Beth gave him an arched-brow look. "Be careful, Uncle Wes, *child spoiler*. What goes around, comes around. Now that you've got a wife, you're bound to have babies of your own. And I've got a long memory."

Hallie felt her face warm at those words, but then her heart squeezed with dread that Wes would say something to indicate he had no plans to have babies with her. She looked at the sleeping infant to conceal her fear, but was taken aback by the emotion that came over her. For a woman who'd rarely even seen babies, this baby was having the most distressing effect on her.

Some deep instinct that she'd never suspected was making itself felt, and suddenly she wanted to touch the sleeping infant, to hold her. What would she feel like? Was her pink skin really as soft and satiny as it looked? And those black curls. They looked as ethereal as delicately spun silk fiber.

"Would you like to hold her?"

Wes's quiet question brought her startled gaze up to his. In that instant she knew her feelings had shown. She searched his dark eyes for any sign that his offer was a token one that he preferred she decline, but she saw nothing but sincerity. As always, self-consciousness held her back.

"Are you sure? I've never held a baby before." She'd included Beth in her glance as she'd said that. Wes had made the offer, but Beth was the baby's mother. Maybe she wasn't so eager to have a near stranger hold her child. She might even be leery of it because Hallie was a Corbett.

"Then sit someplace and get comfortable," Wes told her. "I think I can part with her long enough to give lessons."

Hallie set her handbag on an end table, then chose a spot on the sofa to sit down. Any doubt about Beth's willingness to let her hold the baby was eased when Beth spread a small pad over her lap and grinned down at her.

"It's been a while since her last diaper change. She might leak."

Hallie smiled back. Wes stepped over, then leaned down to hold the sleeping infant over her lap. "She needs her neck and head supported in line with her spine," he said as he placed the baby in her arms. "Meet Natalie Kay Dade."

Hallie went tense, suddenly terrified of the small creature who jerked up a tiny arm and made a fist. Her angelic face twisted into a disgruntled expression, then relaxed. The light weight of her warm little body made Hallie want to cuddle her closer. It was the most amazing feeling.

Wes sat down beside her, his arm over the back of the sofa behind her.

"She's so tiny." Hallie couldn't take her eyes off the sleeping child. She hesitantly touched Natalie's little ankle, then gently stroked the delicate skin, but one touch wasn't enough. She carefully caught the tiny fist between her thumb and forefinger, then smiled when Natalie's fingers opened and latched onto her thumb with a surprisingly tight grip.

Emotion welled up so strongly and unexpectedly that Hallie's lashes went damp. Tenderness sent a sweet gust through her as she was struck by the utter helplessness and innocence of the child. When Natalie made a restless move and opened her eyes to fix almost boldly on Hallie's face, Hallie stared, fascinated by the infant's sober study.

"She's beautiful." Her words were choked with awe. She couldn't resist touching the soft black curls that framed the angelic little face. Natalie's rosebud mouth made a sucking sound and she started to squirm.

"Uh-oh, sis. Where's that bottle?"

As if Natalie had understood Wes's words, she gave a small squeak of distress. By the time Beth went to get the bottle and brought it back, Natalie was making more impatient sounds.

"Hey there, Nattie," Wes said gently. "Let's don't give Aunt Hallie the full treatment today. Give her time to get used to you before you shout the house down."

The husky timbre of Wes's voice drew the baby's gaze and she made an awful face before she gave a baby yell as if defying him. That startled a laugh out of Hallie. The strong impression of personality was evident, deepening Hallie's wonder and delighting her in a way she'd not expected.

Wes took the bottle Beth brought and handed it to Hallie who glanced at Beth for permission. Beth's smiling, "Go ahead," was immediate, and Hallie was touched by her generosity.

Wes showed her how to hold the bottle and Natalie sucked eagerly at the nipple as if she'd been starving. Hallie reveled in every moment of the feeding, including those moments Natalie spent on her shoulder gazing around while she rubbed her back. The gusty little burp of air and the surprise on the baby's face were comical.

Long before Beth whisked Natalie away for a diaper change, Hallie was completely and hopelessly in love. It was a disappointment later when Natalie's eyes fell shut and they put her back in the bassinet for a nap.

The peace and pleasure of the afternoon was spoiled by the phone call from Four C's ranch. Uneasy to be called to the phone, Hallie got up and took the call in the den. Louisa, the maid at the Four C's mansion, was upset.

"Ms. Candice told me and Angel that we were fired and to get our things out of the house this afternoon. She's in a fury, Ms. Hallie. All we know is that you own Four C's. What do you want us to do? Are we fired?"

Hallie gripped the phone, suddenly angry but careful to keep it out of her voice. "No, you're not fired, Louisa," she said calmly, her mind racing for a solution. "But I don't want you to argue with Ms. Candice. I'll come over as soon as I can. In the meantime, follow her order and pack your things. I'll handle it when I get there."

Louisa sounded relieved. "Thank you, Ms. Hallie."

Hallie dropped the phone in its cradle, about to hurry to Four C's when she paused. She walked around Wes's desk to reach the phone book. In moments she'd looked up the sheriff's number and made a call. Then she was on her way upstairs to change her clothes.

As if he knew something was up, Wes came after her. Hallie was shaking with anger and alarm as she hurriedly stripped off her dress.

"What's wrong?"

Hallie glanced at Wes, but went on changing her clothes, too distracted to be self-conscious as she grabbed for jeans and a work shirt to quickly put them on.

"Candice just fired everyone at the house and she's ordered them to pack their things and clear out. I called the sheriff. He's going to meet me at Four C's in twenty minutes."

The moment she'd said Candice's name, Wes had started on his tie, stripping it out of his collar. "I'm going with you."

Hallie stuffed her shirt tail in her jeans and zipped up. She reached for her boots and stomped them on. She moved past Wes to the door and strode across the bedroom for the hall, her nerves spiking higher. The memory of her cousin's red-faced fury in the law office sent ice through her veins.

CHAPTER TEN

THE trouble at Four C's was settled swiftly by the sheriff who mediated everything. Candice had a right to live in the house at Four C's another seven days. And though Candice didn't have a right to fire Louisa and Angel, Hallie had some of the ranch hands move the two women's belongings to the bungalow.

Hallie had then taken the two women aside and written them bonus checks to take a couple weeks off so neither of them would have to deal with Candice again. Hallie couldn't relax until the two women were safely on their way to visit their families.

She hadn't seen or spoken to Candice, but the sheriff had, and he'd filled her in on the details before she'd left Four C's. He'd apparently reminded Candice of her position and gently informed her that she was bound by Hank's wishes. He'd also cautioned Candice about any other actions she might take while she prepared to leave Four C's.

By the time Hallie and Wes had returned to Red Thorn, Beth and Natalie had gone home. Dora had held supper for them, but the meal was silent.

The small crisis with Candice emphasized the vast difference between Hallie and Wes. His life had been sane. The normalcy of his close relationship with his sister was worlds different than the twisted, volatile family relationships Hallie had known.

The Corbetts had wronged the Lansings for generations, with covert destruction of property, secret livestock theft, even violence—the list was long and the consequences few.

You're as much a Corbett as any of us, Hank had declared. Though she'd been horrified and repelled by that, Hallie couldn't deny the family legacy she carried just as much as Candice did. And now she'd inherited the symbol of that legacy.

What would it come to now if Candice challenged the Will and Hallie found herself in a legal battle for Four C's? What did Four C's truly represent to her? As a Corbett, she had a right to the ranch, but the joy of finally getting it had been smothered by today's fresh reminder of the true Corbett legacy. Candice's hysterical bid for power had emphasized it. Though Hallie's bargain with Wes to restore the Lansing homestead was a big step toward righting old wrongs, some wrongs couldn't be put right.

Hallie thought about little Natalie. So sweet, so innocent, so helpless and dependent. Just like any baby of Hallie's would be. What kind of mother would she make?

Hallie glanced across the table at Wes. Had he seriously considered having babies with a woman like her? Even without her background, her inexperience and unproved character would make her a risk.

Deep down, her heart welled up with a cry of protest. If there was one thing she was certain of, it was that she would never injure a child. If anyone knew how poisonous and emotionally lethal cruelty and abuse were to a child, it was her. And it had been

Hank who'd done the damage to her psyche. Thanks to her mother, who'd been loving and protective before her death, Hallie'd had the emotional foundation to survive her grandfather's mistreatment.

Her time today with Natalie had given Hallie a glimpse of how hard it must have been for her mother to do that for her. She must have had to fight to do it. Though Hallie's memories of her mother were dim, she remembered feeling safe with her mother, protected. And loved.

A glimmer of instinct and self-confidence came to her then. She would be a good mother, a tender and loving one. But as she again glanced over at Wes, who had leaned back with his coffee and was staring thoughtfully out the big windows of the dining room toward the patio, she worried that she'd never have a chance for motherhood.

She couldn't imagine loving any man but Wes, but if he couldn't love her, if he didn't want to be married to her, her hunger to love and be loved, to have a true family would come to nothing. She'd never have a child. All she'd have was Four C's.

Before, Four C's had been the zenith of everything she'd ever let herself want, the material symbol of home, or at least a place to belong. She hadn't allowed herself to acknowledge how deeply she'd craved love because it wasn't something she'd realistically believed could ever be hers.

Until Wes. He'd exposed her heart's hungers and he'd given them focus. On him. He'd made her feel desirable and cared for. He'd given her things more precious than land or money.

But he hadn't given her everything. He hadn't said he loved her, and now he hadn't made love to her for days. Did he realize how deeply it hurt to be initiated so thoroughly into lovemaking then have it all stop? She almost wished he'd never touched her. Perhaps it would be better not to have known what lovemaking was like when she'd been destined to lose it.

"I—I think I'd like to go to bed," she said quietly, dismayed by the small stutter and the way her hand trembled as she put her napkin beside her plate. Wes's dark eyes shifted to hers and speared deep.

"I'll be up in a while," he said, but nothing in his voice or in his eyes gave her a hint that he was eager to join her. It was simply an automatic response to her quiet announcement.

Hallie went upstairs, then took her shower. She was still alone by the time she finished and put on a summer nightgown, then got into bed. Within the next five minutes, Wes came in and walked straight to the bath for his shower.

Hallie lay tensely, waiting. She couldn't take this suspense, she couldn't stand not knowing how Wes felt about her or what he would do next. It was better to have a clear answer now and make as clean a break from him as possible. If he didn't want her, she shouldn't be lying next to him at night, harboring impossible hopes.

It startled her when she felt the sting in her eyes dissolve into tears. Impatient with herself and mortified, she rubbed them away. She never cried in front of anyone. Except for a handful of days ago when

Wes's lovemaking had made her cry for joy, she never showed tears.

Never. But the pressure in her chest was hot and turbulent and suddenly it wasn't enough to rub the tears away with her bare hands. She pressed the edge of the sheet to her eyes to get control. It was barely a second after she recovered and lowered the sheet that Wes stepped out into the dim bedroom and flicked off the bathroom light to plunge the room into near darkness.

He walked around to his side of the bed and got in. He settled inches from her. She squeezed her eyes closed in hurt and disappointment when all she felt of him was the male heat that radiated across those inches to her. It took her a while to work up her courage.

"Wes?" she asked softly. "I need to know...." Her heart was fluttering with pain and dread and she had to force herself to go on. "Four C's is mine. I promised you the homestead."

She went silent again, unable to ask the question that made her heart shake with dread: *What do we do now?* "Whether you want me to stay or not, I need—" *Something from you.*

Something from you, Wes. Words she couldn't say. She wanted to be close to him again, in whatever way he allowed. If she could only have sex, she knew now that she'd take it and hope that somehow it would be enough for her. She'd make it everything she could for him.

Because she was too weak to hold out for the pretty words that should go with lovemaking, for the pledge of love a wife had a right to expect from her husband. Maybe he'd feel like saying them someday. Maybe someday she'd have the courage to say them first.

Wes's low voice was deep and quiet. "What do you need, Halona?"

Hallie turned toward him before she realized it, her body so hungry for the feel of him that she didn't know if she could stand it. "I need..."

Emotion was her enemy. It robbed her of her voice but it wouldn't subside. Her hand inched toward Wes in the darkness and her fingertips lightly touched his bare chest.

He lifted his hand and caught hers gently. It was enough of an invitation that she slid closer and slowly, aching with longing and terror, she leaned over him and pressed her lips tentatively to his. Wes's hand curved around the back of her neck to pull her lips harder against his and he took over, devouring her mouth until she could barely hold herself up.

He seemed to know that and broke off the kiss to repeat, "What do you want, Halona?"

Her breathless, "You," sent a spear of fear and regret through her, but she had to take this chance. "You. I want you. I want to touch you, I want you to touch me."

She bit her lip so hard she tasted blood. Lots of it. She couldn't tell him she loved him, she couldn't bring herself to say it. The agony of his silence made her chest pound with pain. She was on the verge of begging him to love her, on the edge of throwing away her dignity to blurt out her love for him.

Halona Corbett could never take that risk. Halona

Lansing was in such turmoil she couldn't wait another second for him to respond to what she'd just said. She pulled away from him and stumbled from the bed so quickly that she never knew if he reached for her or not.

The loud ring of the telephone on the bedside table made Hallie jump. She heard Wes snatch the receiver and rap out a terse, "Lansing Ranch," that was angry enough to make her glance his way in the dark. His fervent swear word and his rushed, "We'll be right there," sent a sobering arrow of alarm through her.

Suddenly the lamp was on and Wes was swinging his legs out of bed. His dark eyes were turbulent as they shot to hers. "The main house at Four C's is on fire, along with several of the barns."

Hallie couldn't move for a handful of seconds. Wes reached her, catching her arm and starting her with him to the closet for clothes.

His fervent, "That damned Candice," sent a wave of sickness through her.

Hallie dressed with hands that couldn't move fast enough. She'd just straightened from getting on her boots when Wes stepped close and caught her chin.

His gruff, "You've bit hell out of that lip," somehow shamed her. She pulled away and stepped back, unable to break contact with the anger and torment that showed so plainly in Wes's dark eyes. His much gentler, "Hurry, baby," was both consolation and apology.

Hallie slipped to the bathroom, quickly rinsed her lip, then grabbed a hair tie before she rushed out.

*   *   *

Four C's ranch hands were clearly fighting a losing battle to save the huge, plantation-style ranch house at Four C's. The moment Hallie and Wes arrived, she was alarmed by the amount of water they were pumping on the flames.

Too shaken to worry that she'd grabbed the arm of her foreman to get his attention, Hallie asked, "Where's Candice? Is everyone out of the house?"

Bob Zane turned to her. "Miz Candice got out safe, there's no one inside."

Hallie leaned closer to shout over the sound of flame and commotion. "You're sure?"

Bob nodded emphatically. Hallie released his arm to look at the ranch mansion. A half dozen men with hoses were trying to douse the flames, but the size of the fire—the size of the house—was too much. The county fire department hadn't arrived yet with their fire engines and water supply.

Hallie glanced toward the ranch buildings where smaller fires were being extinguished. Huge embers from the big house were drifting dangerously over the rest of the ranch headquarters. Hallie gritted her teeth and took a quick breath of the smoke-tinged air as she turned back to her foreman.

"Let the big house burn."

Bob Zane's eyes rounded with a surprise that made her heart fall, but Hallie repeated the words urgently. "Let the big house burn. We've got stock to water and I don't want the wells emptied. Send the men over to wet down the roofs where the sparks are going."

Bob gave a nod, his dark eyes somber and respectful. "Yes, ma'am. Sorry we didn't catch the house sooner." And then he was off, shouting at the men with hoses, organizing them as the water was shut off and the hoses were relocated to the vicinity of the other ranch buildings.

Hallie turned back to stare at the house. The conflagration was loud and violent and terrifying as, without water, it swiftly built into an inferno that washed everything in eerie orange and red light. She lifted her fingers to her mouth and pressed, unable to tear her gaze away as the flames licked viciously at the house.

Wes's big hands slid around her waist from behind. She welcomed the feel of him as he pulled her back against him and pressed his lean jaw against hers. His gruff, "It was the right choice," eased her doubt. "I'm sorry, Halona."

She dropped her hands from her face and rubbed her fingers along the hard-muscled forearms at her waist. She gripped them and pressed her cheek a bit harder against his. She reached up a hand to his jaw and turned her face so only he could hear. "I don't think I'm...sorry."

The words were a confession of her peculiar feelings about the destruction of the main house. She didn't understand it, couldn't yet define precisely why, but she felt only mild disappointment that the beautiful old house was going up in flames.

Wes's arms tightened and he looked down at her. For a long moment they stared at each other before Wes gave a faint nod.

Three county fire engines blasted down the drive

then roared to a stop that placed them in a semicircle around the doomed ranch mansion. The sheriff arrived with two other squad cars behind his cruiser. The house was almost gone by then. All the county fire department could do now was douse the last of the flames and check the other buildings of the headquarters.

Hallie was so caught up in her dark memories of the years she'd lived in that house and her startling lack of regret over its loss that she was slow to react to Wes's low, "Look there." He tightened his arms and gave her a tiny shake. "Halona?"

She turned her head, then followed the direction of his nod to see the sheriff ushering Candice to one of the squad cars. They were flanked by two of the deputies. Candice balked as they reached the back door a deputy had opened. The sheriff took her arm, but when she turned with a doubled fist to swing at him, the two deputies caught her. She was cuffed in seconds, then placed in the car.

Hallie didn't realize she'd pulled away from Wes and was striding swiftly to the squad car until Wes fell into step beside her. She sent him a panicked glance, then stepped up her pace.

The sheriff intercepted them before they reached the squad car. Hallie looked up at the sheriff's grim expression, suddenly so sick that she felt faint. "Oh, God, she didn't..."

"I'm sorry, Miz Lansing. We've got a half dozen witnesses, so I have to take her in." The sheriff's attention shifted to Wes. "I'll keep you posted." And then he turned away, joining his men, giving orders to the deputy who would transport Candice to jail.

Hallie turned dizzily toward what remained of the main house. Delayed reaction to the fire hit her full force. The ranch yard was lit more normally now by the usual night lighting. The blackened ruin where the house had been seemed so much smaller than she'd expected. The ranch mansion that had been home to four of the five generations of Corbetts was little more than drenched rubble.

She heard Wes speaking to Bob Zane, but she didn't follow what either of them said. Eventually, she was able to look away from the ruin to the buildings and barns that made up the rest of the ranch headquarters.

Hallie turned to Wes, and he stopped his conversation with Bob to give her his complete attention. Her quiet, "I need to look things over," got his instant, "I'll go with you." She lifted a hand to his arm and gave it a squeeze. Her voice was a whisper, "I'd like to have some…time. Please."

Wes put his hand over hers, his dark eyes searching her face. "I'll be here. Take all the time you want."

That almost made her break down. Somehow she managed to give him a smile she hoped covered the shock and trauma that was deepening by the moment. Before her smile could wilt to nothing, she turned away and walked toward the nearest buildings, wanting to see for herself that none of the small fires had done more than minimal damage, wanting to be satisfied that there were no hot embers laying somewhere to kindle another fire.

It seemed like hours before she felt better, hours before the excitement died down and she went back to where Wes had parked his car. He stood next to it, leaning back against the side, his arms crossed over his chest as he watched her walk toward him.

The sight of Wes, the comfort of seeing his rugged face, sent a soothing breeze through her soul. It felt like an eternity since they'd left Red Thorn to rush here, an eternity since she'd laid next to him working up her courage to ask what would happen next.

She knew now why the destruction of the main house hadn't upset her more. It had symbolized the Corbett legacy, a legacy she felt ashamed of. For her personally, the house had been a place of pain and darkness where she'd never been accepted. She'd exiled herself from it years ago by moving into the bungalow, but it would have always represented something dark to her. She'd never considered living in it, even before she'd found out she'd inherited it. And now that the mansion was gone, she was tasting something that felt a whole lot like a deep, deep release.

The Corbett legacy was now hers to carry on or to change. And since the choice was finally hers, she meant for her family history to take a drastic turn. A new bit of self-confidence came to her as she felt the power of her resolve.

And it was time to find out exactly what the future held for her with Wes. As she walked toward him, she realized that it was time to stop allowing fear to keep her silent, time to speak her heart, time to settle things with him. The outcome might very well devastate her, but she was weary of the suspense, weary of waiting for someone else to decide what she could have in life.

She'd told Wes that first day that she couldn't stand by and do nothing to get Four C's, but now, she couldn't stand by and do nothing to keep him. She wasn't certain what she could do, but she'd managed to find a husband when she'd thought she had to have one to get Four C's. Surely she'd think of some way to keep the husband she didn't want to lose.

But first she had to know where she stood, and she suddenly couldn't wait another moment to find out.

Wes's bourbon-dark voice was low and sensual in the night air that was still tinged with the smell of wood smoke. "You all right?"

Hallie stopped in front of him and looked up into his eyes. The intensity that had so distressed her those first two days with him was welcome now. He was perceptive enough to sense what was coming, and she felt a little less edgy when his gaze softened and he reached up to trail a callused finger down her cheek. Hallie lifted her hand to press his palm to her jaw.

"You told me you liked it when I talked to you straight out," she said, untroubled that her voice trembled. These might be the hardest words she'd ever speak in her life, the most risky, but she meant to get them out, however they sounded.

Wes straightened until he loomed over her. His face had gone somber.

"I know we married for land," she went on, "that it was a bargain, that love wasn't meant to be part of it. I know we planned that it would end." Her voice broke on that last word and emotion rose so high that it clogged her throat and gave her eyes a painful sting. Wes's face had blurred so much that she couldn't read his expression, but she made herself go on.

"I know what Candice has done tonight might be a scandal you want to distance yourself and the Lansing name from, but I love you now." She had to stop to draw a breath. She was shaking all over.

"I— If it's possible, I want this marriage to be permanent. What I feel for you—"

Sudden nervousness burst out of her in an edgy little sound that was almost a laugh. "I want children, but I know even better than you what my background is, that you might be better off with a more sophis—"

The words were startled out of her when Wes grabbed her arms. She reflexively lifted her hands to his chest, but then his mouth came down on hers and she instantly went weak.

Somehow she got her hands up his shirtfront to wind her arms around his neck, and she clung to him as his mouth mated aggressively with hers. It was a very carnal, deep kiss, so fiery and voracious that she felt her head spin. Her knees wouldn't hold her up.

And yet she whimpered when he eased away. She was breathless, but Wes was, too. She looked up into his face and saw a fierceness about him that she now recognized as passion. He couldn't have kissed her like that if he meant to end their marriage. Her wildly beating heart began to lighten and lift.

"I love you, Halona." Wes's voice was husky and deep, and the sound of it moved through her body like a flood of heavy sweetness. "I didn't mean to give any other impression. I thought you needed time to deal with Hank's death, to decide what you felt about me without pressure.''

He paused and a tremor went through his big body. ''It's been a long four days.''

He kissed her again, more lightly this time, but just when the kiss was on the verge of going out of control, he drew back and crushed her in his arms. His low words seeped through her hair and heated the shell of her ear.

''We got a rough start, but everything important was there from the first.'' He eased back to look down at her. ''Even if we hadn't made our bargain and married that day you walked in, I would have come after you sometime. You got my attention, and it was as much what I sensed in you as it was the lust.''

He pressed a lingering kiss on her lips. ''And the more I was with you, the more I realized that you were special and rare. A woman with as much courage and steel as she had wounds and insecurities.''

Wes lifted a hand and slid his palm along her cheek. ''And if I weren't already married to you, Halona Lansing, I'd ask you to fly with me to Las Vegas tonight.''

Hallie felt the tears then, her heart soaring so high with love and joy that she couldn't hold back. ''I love you, Wes.'' And then he was kissing her again.

His next words were growled against her lips. ''The rest of this conversation won't have many words, Halona. I think it's time we went home.''

Home. To Red Thorn.

Once they got there, they were too hungry for each

other, too eager to fully express what they felt,
to sleep. It was dawn before they finally lay quietly
in each other's arms, before their joy and excitement
settled into a rich warm glow that would last a
lifetime.

It's hard to resist the lure of the Australian Outback

One of Harlequin Romance's best-loved Australian authors

Margaret Way

brings you

Look for

A WIFE AT KIMBARA (#3595)
March 2000

THE BRIDESMAID'S WEDDING (#3607)
June 2000

THE ENGLISH BRIDE (#3619)
September 2000

Available at your favorite retail outlet.

Visit us at www.romance.net

HROUT

If you enjoyed what you just read,
then we've got an offer you can't resist!

Take 2 bestselling
love stories FREE!
Plus get a FREE surprise gift!

Clip this page and mail it to Harlequin Reader Service®

IN U.S.A.	IN CANADA
3010 Walden Ave.	P.O. Box 609
P.O. Box 1867	Fort Erie, Ontario
Buffalo, N.Y. 14240-1867	L2A 5X3

YES! Please send me 2 free Harlequin Romance® novels and my free surprise gift. Then send me 6 brand-new novels every month, which I will receive months before they're available in stores. In the U.S.A., bill me at the bargain price of $2.90 plus 25¢ delivery per book and applicable sales tax, if any*. In Canada, bill me at the bargain price of $3.34 plus 25¢ delivery per book and applicable taxes**. That's the complete price and a savings of 10% off the cover prices—what a great deal! I understand that accepting the 2 free books and gift places me under no obligation ever to buy any books. I can always return a shipment and cancel at any time. Even if I never buy another book from Harlequin, the 2 free books and gift are mine to keep forever. So why not take us up on our invitation. You'll be glad you did!

116 HEN C24U
316 HEN C24V

Name	(PLEASE PRINT)	
Address	Apt.#	
City	State/Prov.	Zip/Postal Code

* Terms and prices subject to change without notice. Sales tax applicable in N.Y.
** Canadian residents will be charged applicable provincial taxes and GST.
  All orders subject to approval. Offer limited to one per household.
  ® are registered trademarks of Harlequin Enterprises Limited.

HROM00_R   ©1998 Harlequin Enterprises Limited

Your Romantic Books—find them at

www.eHarlequin.com

Visit the *Author's Alcove*

➤ Find the most complete information anywhere on your favorite author.

➤ Try your hand in the Writing Round Robin— contribute a chapter to an online book in the making.

Enter the *Reading Room*

➤ Experience an interactive novel—help determine the fate of a story being created now by one of your favorite authors.

➤ Join one of our reading groups and discuss your favorite book.

Drop into *Shop eHarlequin*

➤ Find the latest releases—read an excerpt or write a review for this month's Harlequin top sellers.

➤ Try out our amazing search feature—tell us your favorite theme, setting or time period and we'll find a book that's perfect for you.

All this and more available at

www.eHarlequin.com
on Women.com Networks

HEYRB1

HARLEQUIN®
Makes any time special ™

HARLEQUIN®
AMERICAN ◆ ROMANCE®

WANTS TO SEND YOU
HOME FOR THE HOLIDAYS!

AmericanAirlines®

LOOK FOR CONTEST DETAILS
COMING NEXT MONTH IN ALL
HARLEQUIN
AMERICAN ROMANCE®
SERIES BOOKS!

OR ONLINE AT
www.eHarlequin.com/hometheholidays

For complete rules and entry form send a
self-addressed stamped envelope (residents of
Washington or Vermont may omit return postage)
to "Harlequin Home for the Holidays Contest
9119 Rules" (in the U.S.) P.O. Box 9069, Buffalo,
NY 14269-9069, (in Canada) P.O. Box 637,
Fort Erie, ON, Canada L2A 5X3.

HARHFTH1

HARLEQUIN®
SUPERROMANCE®

Twins

They're definitely not two of a kind!

THE UNKNOWN SISTER
by
Rebecca Winters

Catherine Casey is an identical twin—and she doesn't know it! When she meets her unknown sister, Shannon White, she discovers they've fallen in love with the same man....

On sale May 2000 wherever Harlequin books are sold.

HARLEQUIN®
Makes any time special ™

Visit us at www.romance.net

HSRTWINS2

⬧ *Harlequin Romance*®

Are you dreaming of a man who's rich and masterful, foreign and exciting…

Don't miss these thrilling sheikh stories from some of your favorite authors starting in August 2000…

His Desert Rose (#3618)
by Liz Fielding
August 2000

To Marry a Sheikh (#3623)
by Day Leclaire
October 2000

The Sheikh's Bride (#3630)
by Sophie Weston
November 2000

The Sheikh's Reward (#3634)
by Lucy Gordon
December 2000

Enjoy a little Eastern promise…

Available at your favorite retail outlet.

⬧ HARLEQUIN®
Makes any time special.™

Visit us at www.romance.net

HRSHEIK

Back by popular demand are

DEBBIE MACOMBER's

Hard Luck, Alaska, is a town that needs women! And the O'Halloran brothers are just the fellows to fly them in.

Starting in March 2000 this beloved series returns in special 2-in-1 collector's editions:

MAIL-ORDER MARRIAGES, featuring
Brides for Brothers and *The Marriage Risk*
On sale March 2000

FAMILY MEN, featuring
Daddy's Little Helper and *Because of the Baby*
On sale July 2000

THE LAST TWO BACHELORS, featuring
Falling for Him and *Ending in Marriage*
On sale August 2000

Collect and enjoy each MIDNIGHT SONS story!

Available at your favorite retail outlet.

HARLEQUIN®
Makes any time special ™

Visit us at www.romance.net

PHMS

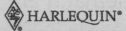
Coming Next Month

#3607 THE BRIDESMAID'S WEDDING Margaret Way
When Ally Kinross and Rafe Cameron meet again at her brother's
wedding, the attraction between them is as powerful as ever. But
their love affair six years ago ended unhappily, and this time Rafe is
determined not to get hurt....

Legends of the Outback

#3608 WIFE ON APPROVAL Leigh Michaels
Paige was shocked to see Austin again. It was seven years since she'd
called him "husband"—now he was only a client! Except he wanted
to give their marriage another try...or did he just want a mother for
the little girl now in his care?

Hiring Ms. Right

#3609 THE BOSS'S BRIDE Emma Richmond
Claris was Adam Turmaine's assistant, but her job description had
temporarily changed. And if being a stand-in mom was demanding,
then living with her boss was equally so—even if he was irresistibly
attractive....

Marrying the Boss

#3610 PROJECT: DADDY Patricia Knoll
Paris Barbour could see that Mac Weston adored the two children
who had been unexpectedly left in his care—he just didn't know
how to show it! As the new nanny, she was determined to help him
learn to be a daddy—and possibly a husband, too....

Baby Boom